Tales of the Were
Grizzly Cove

Alpha Bear

BIANCA D'ARC

DEDICATION

Many thanks to Valerie Tibbs for checking my Italian. *Grazie mille!*

Special thanks to my editor, Jess, and to my readers, especially Anna-Marie Buchner, Suzanne Henry and Peggy McChesney, who have been both kind and encouraging at every turn. Love you guys!

And most especially to my family, and my Dad, for being my rock of Gibraltar. Thanks for always being in my corner.

CHAPTER ONE

Ursula and Amelia were settling in to their new apartment in their new town, but things were definitely strange here in Grizzly Cove. For one thing, the place was lousy with magic. Shifter magic, if Urse didn't miss her guess, just like her grandmother had told her about.

Nonna Ricoletti had taught her granddaughters all about the unseen world. The sisters hadn't really believed most of what Nonna had told them until they got out into the wider world and realized Nonna wasn't just some crazy old Italian eccentric. No, Nonna was a witch. A *strega*.

And she was a Catholic too, but that was Nonna—a woman full of contradictions. She preferred to see the Catholic mother of God as the Mother of All. And if she mixed a little blasphemy into her daily devotions, in the privacy of her own mind, she figured it was between herself and the divine. No need to get some priest involved.

Ursula missed Nonna, but her grandmother had played a large part in shooing Urse and Mellie out to seek their futures. In this new adventure. And this new place. Teeming with shifters.

Bears, mostly, Ursula thought. She didn't have the strongest nose in the family, but Nonna had sworn they were descendants of one of the strongest of the Italian Alpha bears

1

and his human magic-using mate. Nonna was their great-granddaughter, and the magic had stayed strong in her line, while the shifting talent had passed on to other branches of the family that were now somewhat estranged.

Both Urse and Mellie could sense magic. Mellie was better with potions and kitchen magic, as Nonna called it. Urse was better at straight-up spoken or chanted spellwork. Nonna had taught them as much as she knew, and when they'd progressed beyond her abilities, she'd brought in friends of hers from the magic user community for what she called *visits* but were really tutor time for her granddaughters.

There were more than the average number of mages in their hometown of San Francisco, but Nonna had brought in specialists from far afield, including a few from her native land. She'd spared no expense when it came to her granddaughters' education, and they loved her for it—and for the fact that she was the most loving grandmother a kid could ask for.

It had been hard to leave home—and especially Nonna—but she'd practically forced them to go. Nonna had a bit of foresight and had been known to make the odd prophecy now and again. The girls had learned to listen when she gave them advice, and this time, she'd been adamant. She'd told them that their futures were waiting for them in Grizzly Cove and that they shouldn't be afraid to embrace their destinies.

The fact that she'd been so vague, while at the same time being so forceful, meant that she knew a lot more than she was saying. But that was her burden as a clairvoyant, she'd always claimed. She had to balance how much to reveal of the future with what she called *la forza del destino*, or in English, the power of fate.

Luckily, that particular gift hadn't manifested in either of the girls. Personally, Urse thought it would be a real pain in the ass to know what was going to happen and have to decide how much to say in order to arrange the best outcome. That was a little too much like playing the Almighty for her comfort. She didn't trust herself not to mess it all up by saying too much or too little to the wrong person.

Better such things were left to Nonna. She had years of experience and the purest heart Urse knew. Nonna could handle that kind of pressure way better than either of her granddaughters. Which was probably why that gift hadn't passed to either of them, though Nonna claimed it could manifest later in life.

That was something Urse was definitely *not* looking forward to—if it should ever come to pass.

Thankfully, her thoughts were interrupted by the tinkling bell that hung over the door that led to Main Street. Since they weren't open for business yet, it had to be Mellie returning from her sugar run to the bakery down the street.

"Thank the Goddess! I'm about to starve over here, Mel. Gimme one of those honey buns, right now!" she yelled toward the front of the store.

Urse had been stacking books all day, taking them from the back storeroom to the shelves out front, where she was working on their displays. Mellie was supposed to be helping, but she'd gone AWOL about twenty minutes ago, claiming she was just going to make a quick run to the bakery to get snacks.

"I would if I could, but I'm afraid I don't have any on me," a deep voice said from the open doorway that led to the front of the store.

Urse jumped to her feet, dusting herself off. She was a mess. *Dammit*. And in front of the hunky mayor of all people.

"Oh, sorry, Mayor Marshall. I thought you were my sister, finally returning from the bakery." She smiled, hoping he didn't notice how messy her hair was, or the fact that she was wearing zero makeup. Great. Just great.

"Call me John. We don't stand on ceremony around here all that much."

Except for maybe full moon ceremonies, she thought privately. She and Mel were still arguing over whether or not to come clean to the shifters about who they were and what they knew. Urse thought they should tell someone—probably the sexy mayor—before they went any further. If the shifters in town didn't want two *strega* in their midst, that was their right, and Urse certainly didn't want to stay where they weren't welcome. She might be doing all this backbreaking work setting up the store for nothing.

But Mellie didn't agree. She wanted to keep their secret a little longer. She was enjoying ogling the handsome shifters a little too much, if you asked Urse. Of course, nobody was asking her, and Urse didn't want to go against her sister's wishes.

Urse was trying to talk her around, and for the moment, they were at a stalemate.

Continuing with her work, in order to hide the real direction of her thoughts, Urse bent to pick up a heavy box of books. She was just getting her hands under the edge of the box, when two much bigger hands appeared beside her, shooing her away. John lifted up the cardboard box that felt like it was stuffed with anvils—Urse had tried to lift it before—like it was loaded with feathers.

"Where do you want this?" he asked casually.

"Just up on the workbench, please," she said, unable to keep herself from admiring the way his muscles stretched out the fabric of his shirt sleeves. *Hoo-boy.* The man was built!

And those sexy brown eyes that flashed with intelligence just made her heart go pitter-pat. His lustrous golden brown hair made her want to run her fingers through it too. She and Mellie had drooled over the mayor when they'd first met him, and the reaction hadn't faded. The man certainly made an impact on Urse every time she saw him. One she tried hard to tamp down.

The rumor mill around town—aka the Baker sisters who owned the shop down the street—said that the mayor was single, but Urse feared the Alpha shifter wouldn't want to get involved with a witch. Plus, there was the fact that he didn't seem to realize that she and her sisters weren't entirely human. That would have to come out, eventually, but… Oh, it was just so complicated.

John tossed the box easily to the workbench and stood back, just looking at her. She didn't know what to say, which was unusual for her. Urse was usually the more glib-tongued of the two sisters. But there was something about the way he was looking at her.

Their eyes met...and held. Time seemed to stand still. The earth seemed to stop spinning. Just for a moment.

And then, the bell out in the front of the store rang cheerfully, and the world started turning again.

"Hey, Urse!" Mellie yelled on her way into the store. "I got the honey buns. Damn, those Baker sisters got lucky with their shifter mates. I can't decide which one is hotter—or cuter when they're running to keep up with their gals. I've never seen so many shifters in *lurve* before—" Mellie's explosion of words ceased the moment she stepped into the back room and realized they weren't alone. "Oh, crap," she blurted out, coming to an abrupt halt in the doorway. "Hi, Mayor Marshall." The last came out on a squeak.

John looked from Urse to Mellie and back again. "And just what would you two know about shifters?"

Urse sighed heavily and leaned back against the work bench. "More than you might think," she said, knowing this looked really bad. "And *this* is why I said we should tell them," she railed at her sister, who stood silently in the doorway.

"Tell us what, exactly?" John wanted to know.

He didn't look happy, nor could Urse really blame him. This town was his baby, from all accounts. He led the town council. They were able to ratify and deny applications for new businesses, and they were damned choosey about who they let into their community. Urse didn't blame them one bit.

"We are *strega*," Urse admitted, just wanting the truth out there.

"What's a *strega*?" John countered.

Hmm. She hadn't realized he wouldn't recognize the term. She tried again.

"We're hereditary witches from Italy. In the States, I think you would call us magic users or mages," Urse explained. John's brows furrowed as he frowned. "But we're not affiliated with any formal group or school in the U.S. We're solitary practitioners, for the most part, with the traditions passed down through the family. We learned our skills from our grandmother, who shares our gifts, and from special friends she invited to teach us from time to time. But most importantly, we serve the Mother of All and are on the side of Light."

"Well, that's the only good thing I've heard so far." John sighed, running a hand through his hair. Clearly, he was upset.

"We're also descendants of Francisco the Great and his mate, the *strega* Violetta," Mellie put in helpfully. "Francisco was a Marsican bear shifter and protector of the Apennine during the dark times of the Destroyer."

"That was a long time ago," John said, looking at Mellie. "But it speaks in your favor that you're descended of a bear, even if you can't shift." He looked back at Urse, meeting her gaze. "You can't shift, can you?"

"No. Francisco's gift passed to another branch of the family. Our line took after his mate, Violetta," Urse admitted. "Look, John, I'm sorry. I wanted to talk to you about all of this as soon as we realized practically everyone in town was a shifter. On our first visit, we figured we just ran across a random group of shifters, and the rest of the town would be human. Only after we started moving in did we realize what we'd walked into here. I apologize for not telling you sooner."

"Why didn't you?" John surprised her by asking.

Mellie had the grace to blush. "That was my fault," she admitted bashfully. "I liked being around your people, and I wanted to stay for a while before you kicked us out."

"What makes you think I'm going to kick you out?" John said in a quiet voice.

"Well, aren't you?" Mellie looked up at him with those big brown eyes that had been getting her out of trouble since they were kids.

John sighed again. "Hell if I know. This isn't anything I was expecting, and frankly, I'm not sure what to do about it. We started this town for shifters. We only just agreed to let a few humans in. We never even considered magic users would want to join us here, and we haven't made any plans with that situation in mind."

"I'm sorry we've caused trouble for you," Urse said calmly. "If you want us to leave, we will. We should have come clean when we first realized what this place was really all about."

"Yes, you should have," John agreed. "But you're here now. And you already know about us. I think you should just continue setting up your shop. We're going to have to have a meeting, and I'd like you both to be available if the council needs to hear more about your origins, abilities and loyalties. For now, though, just...carry on, I guess." He ran that hand through his thick hair again, clearly frustrated. "I'll be in touch. Don't go near the water and don't go into the woods. Stay in town. Okay?"

"All right, John. We'll do as you ask." Urse walked with him toward the doorway as Mellie moved aside to let him pass. "Please accept my apologies. We should have told you a lot sooner."

John paused in the middle of the store. "You should have. I expect honesty from my people. If you stay, I'll expect that from both of you from now on. Clear?"

His gaze pinned Mellie first.

"Crystal," Mellie replied quickly, hands behind her back as she fidgeted under the weight of that intimidating Alpha male stare.

John turned his attention to Urse, seeking her agreement. She wasn't as intimidated by his gaze. If he was an Alpha male—and she was certain he was—then she was probably the witch equivalent of an Alpha female. She could stand up to a guy like him and not sweat it. Though she didn't feel like opposing John. No, not at all. She felt more like standing with him. By his side.

Now where did *that* odd thought come from? She almost shook herself. On very rare occasions, she almost felt as if an inner bear spoke to her, down deep inside. That furry hussie was seeing something she really, *really* liked when she looked at the mayor. But it was more than just sexual attraction. The beast hidden way down deep saw someone she could trust. Someone who should be respected.

If it was some long-lost ancestral trait, or merely instinct, Urse had learned to trust the female intuition—or bear sense—when it decided to speak to her. Come to think of it, that feeling had become more common since they'd moved. Maybe something about Grizzly Cove was awakening that part of her lineage? Or maybe…it was contact with John that was doing it. Either way, she would pay attention.

"Honesty, John. Now and forevermore," she intoned, knowing some of her magic was leaking out into her words. That happened sometimes.

John started, looking deep into her eyes. He seemed to recognize the vow she'd just made—and reinforced with her own power. Maybe he recognized the kindred bear spirit that was awakening inside her? Or maybe that was all just her imagination.

"Good." He nodded once. "I'll be in touch soon."

He turned and strode forcefully out the door, turning right onto Main Street. She watched until he disappeared from view.

"Holy crap, I'm sorry," Mellie whined, cringing as she looked at Urse.

"Yeah, me too." Urse said, slapping the dust from her jeans. "That could've gone a whole lot better, but at least he didn't try to bite one of us."

"That is one scary bear," Mellie agreed, watching the street where John had disappeared.

"He's the Alpha. Of course he's scary, but lucky for us, he's as controlled as he is powerful. Otherwise, we'd be toast. As it is, I'm not sure they're going to let us stay."

"I'm really sorry." Her sister tried looking pathetic, but Urse wasn't buying it.

The way she saw it, they had a really slim chance of the town council being willing to let them stay, now that the cat was out of the bag. Why that disappointed her so very much, Urse wasn't exactly sure, but she suspected it had a lot to do with the Alpha male who had just walked out the door…and possibly out of her life, for good.

Damn. That was a really shitty thought.

John fumed as he stalked down Main Street toward his office. Of all the things the Ricoletti sisters could have been, mages was right there at the top of the list of no-no's. Shifters didn't mix with other magical races. They barely cooperated among other shifter groups.

John figured he'd been asking a lot of his people to work with the vampire master out of Seattle, but that long-distance relationship seemed to be going well for both sides. They were all still wary, though. He might have established a working rapport with the bloodsucker, but that didn't mean his people trusted the guy.

And the master vampire stayed on his own turf, in Seattle. He didn't come out to Grizzly Cove without specific invitation to view progress on the restaurant in which he was now—rather ironically, since he couldn't ingest food—a silent partner.

But witches…living *in* town? Part of the community? He didn't think his people would go for it. It was one thing to let the odd human in. The three sisters they'd allowed to open a bakery several months before had all ended up mated to bears, so that had worked out really well. With that success under their belts, they'd decided to allow more humans in.

The key word there was *humans*. Nowhere on their business application had the Ricoletti sisters indicated that they were magic users. Of course, that wasn't the kind of thing one just bandied about. Mages were still as secretive as shifters and vamps about their existence. The human world just rolled along…mostly unaware of the magical beings coexisting alongside them.

John liked it that way. Sure, allowing humans to settle in the cove had its risks, but that was why each applicant was so carefully vetted.

How in the world had the witch sisters gotten past the background checks? John didn't know, but he was definitely going to find out. He punched a few numbers into his cell phone as he stalked along Main Street.

The guy in charge of the background checks was also the town's lawyer, Tom. He'd mated recently, to the middle Baker sister, who was also an attorney. She picked up the phone, and John had to school himself not to growl out his frustrations to her. It wasn't Ashley's fault that her mate had been fooled by two Italian-American witches.

"Is Tom there?" John asked, his temper running close to the surface.

"He's at your office, John," Ashley answered promptly. "He had some candidates he wanted to run past you."

John really wanted to growl, but he bit it back. Again.

"Thanks, Ashley. I'll catch him there."

He rang off as politely as he could manage under the circumstances and took the steps into City Hall two at a time. He stomped into his office at the back of the building, and sure enough, there he was. Tom. Asshole of the hour.

"You've got a lot of explaining to do," John said without preamble as Tom stood by the visitor's chair in front of John's desk.

"What's wrong?" Tom asked.

He was one of John's go-to men for a reason. Tom was a problem solver, which was normally something John respected, but Tom had fucked up royally, and John was pissed.

"How about two witches opening a bookstore in the middle of town? And, oh yeah, they recognized all of us as shifters without even breaking a sweat." John paced behind his desk, unable to sit still as his anger peaked.

"What?" Tom looked dumbfounded, then concerned, followed swiftly by anger and a flush of embarrassment.

It wasn't often Tom was caught flatfooted, but John saw all the signs of it now. Damn. He wanted to be angry with his friend and lieutenant, but he knew Tom was a straight shooter. He'd messed up, but he was just as troubled as he ought to be by the situation. Maybe even more so—since it was his fault the *strega* sisters had gotten this far.

"Those nice Ricoletti girls just informed me that they're both magic users. Apparently, they come from a long line of Italian *strega*."

"*Strega*, huh?" Tom looked thoughtful as he obviously recognized the word.

"You know about *strega*?" John countered quickly. He needed reliable information, and he needed it yesterday.

"Yeah, I crossed paths with a *strega* once. A long time ago." Tom's tone turned contemplative. "She saved my life, actually."

That took a bit of the wind out of John's sails. He found enough calm to sit.

"Tell me all," he invited, though it was more like an order.

"It was before I hooked up with your unit, John," Tom began. "Me and two other guys were detached to protect the U.S. ambassador on a trip to Rome. Remember the terrorist attack? I was in the middle of it and took five bullets to the abdomen before we could save the ambassador's bacon and get him out of there. The team assumed I was wearing a vest, but you know how I hate the way those things chafe. I was bleeding, but I told them it was only a graze, and in the confusion of the scene, I got away with it. Until I couldn't anymore. I collapsed in a back alley near the Vatican while pursuing the perps. Our radios were shit with all the chaos and crossed signals, so nobody missed me."

"I knew you were in the thick of that action, but I didn't know you'd been injured," John said, encouraging his friend to go on.

It was clear that Tom was reluctant to talk about whatever

had happened. He was probably embarrassed, but he'd have to get over that. John needed to know what he knew about *strega*.

"A priest found me and somehow recognized what I was. He contacted a woman he knew, and she took me into her home. She was a *strega*. I was pretty far gone. One of the bullets had hit something important, and even with our natural healing abilities, I was close to death. I thought, at the time, that I'd just asked too much of my body, but the lady—the witch—set me straight. One of those bullets had been cursed, she claimed later, and I was in no position to argue. She did some magic, and I woke up in the middle of it. There was a really intense golden light. I could see the woman and the priest through this sheen of the most beautiful light I've ever been exposed to. It felt like the sun—the most intense sun you've ever felt—on a warm summer day. Good and golden and pure."

Tom's eyes had lost their focus on the here and now, and John listened with great interest to the story. He hadn't had a lot of experience with Catholic priests, but John had long held the belief that most people who dedicated their lives to serving their chosen deity in a non-violent way, and helping others, were probably on the right side of things.

It sounded like the priest who had found Tom knew things about the unseen world, if he'd realized Tom was a shifter. The thought intrigued him, but it was for later consideration. What he needed to know about right now was the woman. The *strega*.

"She healed me with her magic. I could feel the bullets popping out of my body and hear them clattering on the floor. I'd counted five hits, but there were more pieces than that coming out of me. Some of those bullets had fragged, which helped explain why I was so badly injured, but even that shouldn't have put me down. I mean, I fell like a rock. Hard. I've never been so out of it before, or since." Tom seemed to reflect for a moment, and John didn't rush him.

He seemed to be remembering things as he spoke about

them, and John could see how difficult it was for him to speak of the events. No shifter—especially not one as strong or capable as Tom—wanted to admit to moments of weakness.

"The lady healed me, and I had to leave as soon as I could walk," Tom went on. "The terrorists were still out there, and my team was hunting them. I had to get back to the fight, which was ongoing. I realized as I came out of it completely that only about forty minutes had passed. The priest gave me a quick briefing of what he knew, and I listened in on the confused comms that were coming through my radio. The scene was still chaos, and I needed to get back out there. The priest blessed me, if you can believe it, and the woman added her own little sparkle of magic as I took off and helped track down the bad guys."

"Is that it?" John asked when Tom trailed off again. "Is that all you know about *strega?*"

Tom shook himself and focused on John. "No, sorry. As you know, we caught the terrorists. After that, I went back to the lady's house to thank her. She invited me in for coffee, and we talked. She told me a little bit about her calling. She said that *strega*, like all people, can be good or bad, but that because of where she lived, so close to the Vatican, pretty much every *strega* in the area was working on the side of Light. In fact, they'd congregated there to take advantage of the good juju coming off the concentration of spiritual thought and prayer coming out of that area. A few special priests were aware of the *strega* and their magic. The one who had brought me to her was one of them. She clearly had great respect for the man, and she told me where to find him. After I left her, I went straight to the little church where she told me I'd find the priest, to thank him. He invited me into his home for another cup of coffee, and I was intrigued enough to accept his invitation."

Tom reached for his cell phone, hitting a few buttons before he went on. "I have his number, and the lady's. I could call either of them—or both—and ask about the

Ricolettis. I have a feeling the *strega* working on the side of Light all know each other, or at least know *of* each other."

"You keep in touch with them still?" John was impressed by that. Clearly, those two people had made a larger impression on Tom than John had realized.

"We talk occasionally. Mostly around the holidays. Just friendly greetings. Antoinetta calls me once in a while, if she has a shifter question, and she's invited me to do the same if I have a magic problem. So far, I haven't taken her up on it, though I've been meaning to call and tell her I found my mate and maybe ask what she might know about sea monsters." Tom looked at John questioningly, as if seeking his input.

John thought about it for a few seconds. "Are you sure you're comfortable with these people knowing about your mate?" Mates had to be protected at all costs. The fact that Tom had found his was too precious to take lightly.

"I trust them both with my life. They saved me once. I doubt they would do anything to me or anyone I claimed as mine. In fact, I see them both as allies. They would help me and mine, if they could."

"You're that sure about them?" John was surprised by Tom's vehemence.

Tom nodded. "Sure as I can be." He paused before continuing. "You didn't experience that golden light, John. There was no way either of them could ever be evil, in any way. What I felt that day as they saved my life was a truly spiritual experience. Oh, and most *strega* follow the Goddess, though Antoinetta hides her devotion behind Catholic traditions. She has a beautiful shrine in her garden with a statue of a woman at its center."

"All right. Make the call. Do you think she would mind if you conferenced me in?" John asked. This was Tom's contact. John would let Tom decide how best to handle the connection.

"I think she'd enjoy it," Tom said, smiling as he dialed the number. "Luckily, it's not too late to call where she is." Tom put the call on speaker, and John heard the phone start to ring on the other end.

What followed was one of the strangest conversations John had ever had. Tom greeted the lady in Italian, then switched to English as he introduced John. Antoinetta's English was excellent, though heavily accented. She seemed a warm person, the kind whose friendliness reached right through the phone lines and into the room. Magic? John wasn't sure, but his instincts told him she was all right.

She explained what she could about Italian *strega* in general, but wouldn't say too much until she knew why John was asking. John could respect that. She didn't know him, and even with Tom vouching for him, she was right to be cautious. With the strange goings on in the world today, the magical races had to be on alert.

"I understand your hesitancy," John said patiently, hoping to convince the woman to speak more candidly. "We know the world is becoming even more dangerous than it was. We've been warned that the *Venifucus* are on the loose, running around, trying to bring back their former leader." John threw that out there to see what the woman might say.

"If what I believe is true, they already have," Antoinetta intoned rather ominously.

"What?" Tom jumped on the statement. "Do you know this for certain?"

"No, my friend. I'm sorry. It is a vision by one of my sisters. She sometimes sees things, but I have no concrete evidence as yet. She saw fire and smoke. Lightning and ash. And a woman, the Destroyer, come through in the heart of flame."

"We know for a fact that they were trying to siphon the power from at least two volcanoes and the San Andreas fault to open the rift between worlds," Tom told her. "In each of those cases, shifters stopped the *Venifucus* agents before they could do too much damage."

"Let me guess." Antoinetta's voice sounded a bit mischievous. "Iceland. That had to be the white tiger, right?

15

And maybe that mountain up near where you live, in the Pacific Northwest? Did you have something to do with that, my friend?"

"Not me," Tom explained. "But definitely folks like us."

"That leaves South America," Antoinetta said, a bit of solemnity returning to her voice. "Or here, in my homeland. I will have to look into this further, but if what my sister saw is true—and I have no reason to doubt her—then we are in for a rough ride as soon as the Destroyer recovers from her journey. It is no easy thing to travel between realms. Even for one of her power, it will have weakened her. She will not want to show herself to the world until she has regained her strength. And then…"

"And then, all hell breaks loose," Tom completed the thought.

Silence reigned for a moment before John got back into the conversation.

"With your permission, I'm going to tell the Lords of our kind here in the States about this," John said politely. Truthfully, he'd pass on the woman's words with or without her okay, but he preferred that she knew he was going to tell them.

"Thank you," Antoinetta surprised him by saying. "I don't want to alarm anyone, but we should all be wary until we know for certain." John sat back in his chair, pleased with the way the conversation was going. "Now, as for your *strega*," she went on. "What are their family names? Perhaps I know their people."

"They're sisters. Their family name is Ricoletti," John said, surprised by his own hesitancy. He didn't want to cause trouble for the sisters, and somehow, he felt protective of their privacy—which made no sense.

"Ricoletti! Why didn't you say so?" Antoinetta made some tsking sounds in the background. "They come from a long line of well-respected *strega* and ones like you." She trailed off for a moment, then returned triumphantly. "Maria Ricoletti was a friend of my grandmother. She married an American and moved to San Francisco after the great war. Her daughter was not blessed with the family gifts, but Maria said her granddaughters were carrying on the Ricoletti name and heritage. They were born with their father's last name, but took the Ricoletti name when they took their place as *strega*. It's how we all keep track of each other. Women with the gift take on the name of the family line that trains them. It was easier in the old days when we all had so many names and no computers to keep track of every little detail," she groused.

"So they were telling the truth about being descended from a bear named Francisco?" John asked.

"Oh yes. Francisco was a great hero. He and his mate, Violetta, stood against the Destroyer, successfully defending a great swath of Italy from the *Venifucus* and their leader. They were secret allies of the Holy See, and between the two, Italy fared as well as any land could during that dark time. It was much worse for our northern neighbors. Without Francisco and Violetta, we would have been as ravaged as the rest of Europe."

CHAPTER TWO

John was surprised by what he was hearing, but it was a pleasant sort of surprise. Maybe...just maybe...they had found new allies in the unexpected arrival of the witchy sisters, instead of more problems.

"I'm glad to hear this," he told the Italian lady honestly. "I didn't expect we would have magic users in our community, but if they're here, it's important that they be on the right side of things. We're sworn to serve the Lady and her Light," he admitted, showing Antoinetta a modicum of trust.

"And I am pleased to hear that as well. If my sister's vision is true, all of us who are on the side of Light will have to work together in the coming times," she said, echoing the words of the Lords of all *were*creatures.

"So our leaders have told us," John agreed. "And so I believe. Though I didn't expect it to happen quite so fast, or just this way. Which brings me to my final question." He needed to know if this woman knew anything about sea monsters—strange at that sounded, even in the privacy of his own mind. Nevertheless, he launched into the story of Master Hiram's yacht being chomped on by some giant sea creature a few weeks ago, and the subsequent tentacle-attack on one of the Baker sisters while she was walking near the water. He asked what Antoinetta knew of such things.

"I have heard tales of the leviathan," she said quietly, surprising him yet again. "Such creatures as that which attacked the woman in your town were known in ancient days, and they are not of this realm. They are evil and ruled by the one known as the leviathan. That is the largest of them all, and if it is banished, so are all its minions. It sounds like the big one attacked the yacht. A minion tried to kill the woman on the beach. Sadly, I have heard stories like this from our own coasts earlier this year, though the activity has died down a bit now. The leviathan is a magical creature and can cross vast oceans quickly. It is attracted to magic. It probably sensed the concentration of your people in the area and came to see if it could feed. Whatever you do, keep your people out of the water. It will attack any tasty magical target, though the leviathan goes after only the most powerful. Its minions will try for smaller prey."

"Good to know," John said, frowning. Everything Antoinetta said made sense. A creepy, rage-inducing sort of sense. John was angry that something was actively hunting his people. "Is there anything that can stop the leviathan?" He would make it happen. He would keep his people safe.

"I am sorry to say, such things are probably beyond the power of people like you and me, Alpha. This would require a specialist. Someone—or, more likely, a team of magical beings—with power over the oceans and the creatures within. Do you know any selkies? Really powerful ones?"

"Maybe…" John was thinking fast, wondering who he could call on to help with his sea monster problem.

"I will see if there are any good sea witches operating near you and put you in touch, if you wish. You need specialized help. Do not try to engage the leviathan on your own. Many good men and women have fallen to it over the centuries, but it was banished before. Something freed it now. Probably *Venifucus* agents. But if we get the right kind of power arrayed against it, it can be banished again."

"Can't it be killed?" Tom asked.

"Sadly, no. Not in this realm. It is not of this place, and it is still tied to its place of origin. Or so it is believed. It can be sent back there, but not killed here while its being resides elsewhere—half-in and half-out of our plane of existence."

"I think that's above my pay grade, but an interesting problem," Tom said with a grim chuckle. "Would a priestess help?"

"Perhaps…" Antoinetta seemed to think about it. "It couldn't hurt to have someone casting protective spells on your side. It might at least prevent attacks like what happened to that girl walking on the beach. You could ask the Ricolettis to help. They would easily be able to cast such wards."

"Do you think we can trust them?" Tom asked. John wouldn't necessarily take the word of this woman he'd only just met by phone, but Tom knew her and obviously trusted her.

It spoke well of her that she'd saved Tom's life, and for that reason, John was giving her words a lot more weight than he normally would on such short acquaintance.

"Ricolettis? Of course, you should trust them. They are one of the oldest and most respected families in our tradition. Those girls would not have been granted the privilege of using that family name without first proving their worth. They've been tested and trained by the best. They are on the right side of things. The Ricolettis have always served the Light." Antoinetta's tone was one of shock that such a thing would even be questioned, but then again, she knew all about the Ricoletti heritage.

The idea of families passing down those kinds of traditions was foreign to John. Sure, shifter cubs were born of shifter parents, but free will dictated how each child would turn out—much like with humans. There were good and bad shifters, though most were taught respect and worship of the Goddess. But some chose other paths, and John had learned to judge each shifter on his or her own merits and actions.

"Thank you for speaking so freely with us," John said politely, meaning every word. He sensed a new alliance might be in the works, and if Antoinetta's dire predictions came true, alliances of every shape and size would be needed in the days to come. "If you ever travel to the States, I hope you'll consider paying a visit to Grizzly Cove."

"I am honored by the invitation, Alpha," Antoinetta said with due respect. She probably knew what a big step it was for him to invite her into his domain. "And if you ever find yourself in Italy, I hope you will visit with me. I would love to meet the man strong enough to earn Thomas's loyalty."

John could hear the true admiration in her voice for Tom. That earned her a few brownie points as far as John was concerned. He surrounded himself with strong bears on purpose. His men made him a better leader. Their excellence kept him striving to be better—to be worthy of being their leader.

They ended the call after exchanging a few more pleasantries, and Tom shared his big news about finding his mate, to suitable jubilation from his *strega* friend. Tom had managed to surprise John with the connection to an honest-to-goodness witch. John had thought he'd known everything about his men and their pasts, but it seemed there were still a few things to learn. In a way, John liked that. It would keep him on his toes.

When Tom finally hit the *end* button on his phone, he sat back and just looked at John, waiting for him to speak. John let him wait while he thought everything through.

"What's your current assessment of Antoinetta's trustworthiness?" John asked in a rapid-fire way that he'd often used as the leader of his Spec Ops warriors. Old habits died hard, it seemed.

"She's true blue, John. She has never steered me wrong, and I still owe her for saving my life. I've kept tabs on her all these years, and she's never done anything to make me question what team she plays for. She's on our side. No doubt in my mind."

The tone of Tom's reply, even more than the words, told John of the strength of Tom's belief in his connection with the foreign witch. It seemed John was going to have to trust to Tom's judgment once again. That wasn't unusual, but after Tom's failure to discover the true nature of the Ricolettis *before* they moved in, it was a little hard to swallow.

"All right." John had made his decision. "We'll follow Antoinetta's advice for the moment. I'm going to ask the Ricoletti sisters to add magical protections to the cove. Depending on how they respond to that request, we'll see where we go from there."

Tom stood, no doubt hearing the dismissal in John's voice. "If you need me to talk to them, I'd like a chance to make up for my mistake. I'm going to add a new requirement to the application process for new residents and business owners. We're going to have to find some way to test them for magic. I hadn't really considered it before, and that's my bad. I'm sorry I failed you, Alpha. It won't happen again."

John appreciated Tom's contrition, but his anger had dissipated during the call to Italy. "Don't sweat it, Tommy. None of us considered the idea that a magic user would actually petition to live here. We all overlooked that, and now, we've learned our lesson. Figure out the best way to unobtrusively have new candidates screened for magic and present your plan at the next council meeting. Nobody new is coming in until this is settled."

Tom agreed and took off, leaving John in his office to think over his options.

There was nothing for it. He was going to have to talk to the Ricoletti sisters again. The problem wouldn't get solved until he started the ball rolling. And if he found his inner bear sitting up and taking interest in the idea that he'd soon see Ursula again, John tried not to notice.

"You've done it now," Urse said to her sister once she'd calmed down. "They're probably going to run us out of town on a rail."

"And you think it would have gone any better if we'd gone to them on bended knee the way you wanted? Either way, they were going to be pissed," Mellie argued unapologetically.

"The way this came out made us look really bad, Mel. It was really embarrassing."

"Oh, get over it, Urse. Mr. Cutey Mayor was going to find out either way. What difference does it make how it happened? Or did you honestly think either of us stood half a chance with a guy like that?" Mellie scoffed.

Her words hurt, striking a little too close to truth for Urse's peace of mind. She bit her tongue, not saying a word, which in itself, spoke volumes.

"Oh, shit, Urse. The mayor? Really?" Mellie's tone was sympathetic, but Urse couldn't stomach her pity right now.

Urse hadn't even really realized that she was interested in John Marshall. Not until the shit had hit the fan, and she'd been outed right in front of him. She'd wanted to dig a hole and bury her head in the sand right then and there, but of course, she couldn't. She'd been stuck there, feeling like an idiot and watching all her half-formed dreams crash around her.

Urse set down the books she'd been sorting and walked out of the shop. She needed air, and she needed to get away from her sister. Mellie had a way of grating on her nerves every once in a while, and this was definitely one of those times.

She heard Mellie call after her, but she couldn't deal with her right now. Urse ignored her as she walked across the street and headed for the picnic area by the beach.

It was empty, of course. Everyone in town had been told to stay away from the beach for some reason that wasn't too clear to Urse, but she didn't care much for vague warnings at the moment. She wanted a little peace, and maybe the wash of the waves would help wash her worries away. At least for a little while.

Urse walked parallel to the shore, listening to the waves, feeling the tears that were a mixture of the action of the wind in her face and, if she was being honest, more than a little regret for those half-formed dreams that would now never be.

She didn't know how long she walked along the beach before she sensed something...wrong. She stopped short and found herself backing away from the shore. There was something really *wrong* out there in the water.

Urse had no idea what it could be, but she knew to trust her instincts, and she started backpedaling as fast as she could, heading back the way she'd come as far up the beach as she could get from the water's edge. All the while, she called on all the protective magics she knew that she could cast quickly and while on the move.

It wasn't the most effective defense in the world, but when the water started churning about twenty feet out into the cove and then stopped short about fifteen feet away, not coming any closer, she was glad she'd thought to cast any wards at all. She was running now, heading back to the picnic area at her top speed, which wasn't all that fast, since she wasn't much of an athlete.

She kept one eye on the water, watching the churning spot follow her progress as she moved back toward the center of town, where she could get off the beach entirely. Unfortunately, she'd walked so far around the cove, she'd stumbled near heavily wooded private property. She feared getting lost in the woods and encountering one of the residents in bear form more than the threat in the water at the moment, so she ran around to where the trees cleared and the town brushed up against the apex of the cove.

As soon as she could run off the beach and into town, she would. Even if the closest route would take her right past city hall...and the mayor's office.

Then again, maybe she needed to stop there and report what she sensed. Now that the cat was out of the bag, it would be irresponsible of her not to report this event to someone. Maybe she could talk to the sheriff. His office was in the same building. She saw the break in the trees drawing closer just as her ward failed, and she made a run for it.

Looking over her shoulder as she ran, she saw massive tentacles reaching out of the water toward her, but with any luck, she'd be out of range. A thundering crash behind her sent up a cloud of sand and shook the ground beneath her as she continued to run.

"Holy shit!" she cursed, even as she ran for her life.

Thank the benevolent Goddess, she was just out of range of that thing. Whatever the *hell* it was! She had no choice but to tell somebody in charge about this incident. She ran for city hall as if the hounds of hell—or at least their *giant freaking octopus* cousins—were on her tail.

"What the hell?" John felt the earth shake as he sat at his desk, contemplating how he was going to approach the Ricoletti sisters.

He stood and rushed out front to the reception area. The sheriff, Brody, was already there, talking on his radio to Zak, his deputy. From the sound of the transmissions, neither of them knew what was going on.

"Earthquake?" Brody offered as he finished speaking with Zak.

"Too short. That was something hitting the ground," John replied as he headed to the window. What he saw when he looked out had his jaw dropping, and then, he sprang into action.

He leapt toward the door and opened it just as Ursula Ricoletti reached it. She ran through without stopping, and he slammed it behind her, looking out at the mess in the water some distance away. No doubt about it, she'd riled something up out there, and it wasn't happy.

But first things first.

"Are you okay?" John snapped out. Ursula was leaning heavily against the front desk, breathing hard. She was definitely winded but looked otherwise whole. "Did it touch you?"

She shook her head, still unable to form words as she tried to recover. John breathed a small sigh of relief, quickly replaced by anger that she'd come so close to being hurt.

"Didn't I tell you to stay away from the water? Dammit,

Ursula, that thing would have loved to snack on you. It's attracted to magic!"

She glared up at him, bent over and breathing hard.

"Nobody said there was a fucking sea monster in the cove!" she rasped out between heavy breaths.

The profanity washed over him and made him step back. She must be really riled to use such language, and that fact apparently wasn't lost on Brody either. John met the sheriff's raised eyebrows and jerked his head, ordering him silently to vamoose.

Brody took the hint and headed outside. "Just going to check the perimeter," he said needlessly as he left.

"Sorry, sweetheart. I didn't mean to berate you," John said gently as he calmed down. She was safe. He had to keep reminding his inner bear, she was safe.

"Well, it would have been nice to know why we were being warned off," she added, starting to catch her breath. "I'm sorry. I was upset with my sister, and I just wanted to take a walk. I didn't think it would be dangerous. Not like that." She straightened and wiped the light sheen of sweat on her forehead with one hand. She smelled of fear and delicate exertion.

While John didn't like the scent of fear on her, his inner bear wanted to bask in the warm scent of her sweat. She smelled like honey and spice to his wilder side, and that kind of thing could easily get addictive.

"It's okay," he said, walking closer to her as they both calmed a bit more. "We argued about what to tell you and your sister when we thought you were human. Now that we know you know about magic..." he trailed off.

"Yeah, now we really need to know about the really pissed off magic sea monster in the cove. In fact, it would have been good to know about this about an hour ago," she quipped, regaining a bit of the humor he'd come to expect from her in their brief encounters.

"I'm sorrier than I can say," John said softly, coming to stand right in front of her. "And I'm glad you're okay. Are you sure it didn't hurt you?"

She chuckled. "You probably should ask if I hurt it," she surprised him by saying, some of her spirit returning. "Give me another crack at that bastard when I'm prepared, and I'll do my best to kick its ass."

John had to chuckle with her. She looked so ladylike, it was kind of nice to learn she had a temper. With the long, wavy black hair, deep brown eyes and a light complexion, she had a sort of Snow White thing going on. She looked very regal and delicate, and absolutely stunning. In fact, John thought she might just be the most beautiful woman he'd ever seen in real life.

Finding out that she cussed when she was scared was amusing. It also made her seem a little more approachable. As did, perversely, her temper. John liked a woman to have fire, and Ursula was showing not just fire but white-hot incendiary flames burned within her, just waiting for an occasion to let loose.

He liked it. And his bear wanted to rub up against her silky long hair and drown in her luscious scent. *Down, boy.*

"You may get your wish," John said, doing his best to focus. He was relieved that she'd brought up the subject he'd been contemplating before her abrupt, and rather dramatic, arrival. "In fact, I was sitting in my office, trying to figure out how to talk to you about this very thing."

She looked up at him, her expression droll. "You're kidding, right?"

"Nope." He smiled at her, feeling his heart lighten for no discernible reason. "Turns out, one of my guys is very well acquainted with one of your people."

"A Ricoletti?"

"No, but she is a *strega*. From Italy. We talked long distance about you and your family, and she vouched for the Ricolettis."

"You don't say?" She looked impressed, and pleasantly surprised.

"I asked this lady about our little sea creature problem,

and she suggested I ask you and your sister to cast some magical protections around the cove, if you're willing." He squinted, realizing he was asking a lot of her on short notice.

Ursula slumped against the desk, leaning back a bit, just looking at him.

"Look, I know it's a big ask, but you've seen what we're up against. The *strega* I just spoke with said it might be a leviathan—an evil, magical creature from another realm that cannot be killed, only contained. I have some specialist help coming—eventually—to try to banish it, but for now, we need some strong magical protections around the cove to try to prevent more attacks on land."

"More? This has happened before?"

"Not quite as dramatically," John replied, smiling a bit. "But yeah. Tina Baker was accosted a while back by a smaller version of what came after you just now. It reached out of the water and twined around her leg. Zak went bear on its ass and ripped the tentacle off. We sent it off for analysis, but we kept a chunk on ice, if you want to see it."

Ursula made a face. "That's probably more my sister's domain, but we should both probably take a look."

"Why would your sister be more interested?" John asked, surprised.

"Oh." She blinked a few times. "Yeah, well, we're all a little...uh...individual in our talents. I'm better at spoken or chanted spellwork. Mellie does potions. She could probably use a little bit of that frozen piece of yuck to work up a counter-spell. I'm your girl for casting wards. In fact, I plan to start as soon as I recover. That thing isn't getting its suckers near anyone else on my watch." She sounded determined, which John respected.

"How about we start tomorrow?"

"We?" She sent him a narrow-eyed look.

"I'd like to be present. We know this thing goes after magic. I didn't get a chance to tell you yet, but the master vampire of Seattle washed up on our shore a little bit ago. The thing that went after you chomped on his yacht and killed his crew. He was really messed up when he got here, but Zak saved him."

"Zak again?" She chuckled wryly. "Seems the deputy gets around. And here I thought he was the little guy in this crowd."

"Never judge a bear by his size. Zak may not be a grizzly, but he's got a heart as big as the world and the guts to match." John believed every word. He'd seen Zak outfight bigger guys and outshoot every man in his battalion. Zak was a dangerous man to underestimate.

Ursula nodded. "Understood. But you don't have to defend him to me. I've been a fan of the deputy's since he welcomed us to the town and asked if we'd be able to find him a first edition of the Silmarillion. The man has discerning tastes. Mellie's been green with jealousy that Tina got to him first."

John laughed outright at that.

"So you want to watch me work?" she asked, shooting him a sideways grin. "I don't mind, I guess. And to be honest, I'd be happy to have backup in case this thing is more than I can handle."

He saw it then—the real terror that must have filled her as she ran from the monster. John followed his instincts and leaned against the desk, by her side. He put one arm around her shoulders and gathered her close. He felt the fine tremor that hadn't left her body and realized she was still feeling the reaction high of running for her life.

"I'll guard you with my life, Ursula. It'll have to go through me if it wants you, and that won't happen easily."

"I don't want you to get hurt either, John," she whispered, turning toward him.

He couldn't resist. He gathered her into his arms, hugging her tight against his chest.

"Ssh. It'll be okay. There's nothing that can touch us if we work together, right? Your magic, my claws. We'll be okay."

"You promise?" The small whisper floated up to him as he stroked his hand down her back, trying to offer what comfort he could.

"You have my word," he replied in a gentle voice.

Little by little, her shaking stopped as she calmed under his touch. Her head fit nicely under his chin, and her warm, curvy body seemed like it was made for his arms.

A dangerous thought.

"You okay now?" he asked, feeling the intimacy of the moment curling around him. It was a pleasant sensation, but one he had to resist.

She had admitted to being a witch. A magic user. Someone he should be wary of, not want to take in his arms and keep...forever.

Oh, no. No, no, no.

John let her go, hoping she would move away before those even more dangerous thoughts of his took hold and moved in to stay. He swatted mentally at his bear half. They could not keep her. She was not for them. She was magic. A witch. Not a shifter. Not even a human. She was a woman of power in her own right, and he had no idea if she could commit to a shifter the way a shifter needed her to commit to build a future.

Shifters needed the bond. If not the sacred and profound mating bond that formed between shifters, then the deep love bond that could form between a shifter and a human mate. But John had no idea what would happen if a mage was added into the mix. Could they feel the bond? Any bond? And could it last a lifetime, or could a magic user walk away, leaving a broken shifter behind, likely to die, all alone and heartbroken?

John did *not* want to be the one to find out.

CHAPTER THREE

Urse was having a hard time calming her racing heart—not only from her run-in with the leviathan, but from the mayor's close proximity. For a moment there…just a moment…she'd thought maybe he was going to kiss her. And then, he backed away.

Was that disappointment flowing through her veins alongside the continued excitement from being so near him? *Nah. Couldn't be. Could it?*

She decided she could be an adult and handle this calmly. *Right?* Okay, maybe not completely calmly, but at least not running around screaming, the way she had entered the town hall. Even if a small part of her wanted to keep on running.

She banished the nerves. They had no place here. Not if she was going to be casting spells and using her magic against…a freaking leviathan! Her knees wanted to give out again, but she hid it by casually leaning back against the desk.

"So. Leviathan, you said?" She pretended to consider, trying to project calm instead of the bone-deep fear that hit her just speaking the word.

"That's what the *strega* in Italy said. There have been rumors of attacks up and down the coast of Italy by smaller versions of what came after you today. Just like what tried to drag Tina under. Baby sea monsters, if you will. But the big daddy seems to be parked here, attracted by the concentration of shifter magic—and your magic too, I guess."

"I don't doubt it," she agreed, thinking as fast as she could. "I should phone my grandmother. She could help me figure out what might work best," she said aloud, thinking hard.

"I'd like to listen in, if you don't mind," John came straight out and said.

Her gaze shot over to him. He was standing several feet away now, looking as grim and unapproachable as she'd ever seen him. If he'd been in bear shape, he would have been bristling at her, she was sure.

Well, she didn't like that one bit. And she wasn't going to back down. He might be a big-ass grizzly shifter, but she was a *strega*, from a proud and ancient tradition. She could take him on any day of the week. Probably.

"You don't trust me to talk to my grandmother?" she lashed out, the whip of aggravation in her voice.

"I don't trust you at all," he countered, knocking her back with the verbal assault. "You've already lied to me—to the entire town—once. You're not the simple humans I thought you were, so forgive me for being wary. In the shifter world, being cautious helps you live longer, and I plan to live a good long time."

"With no friends," she grumbled under her breath as she fumed.

She busied herself by sitting back on the desk, uncaring if she dislodged the pencil cup or the blotter. Her knees were shaking too bad. She couldn't stand, and she couldn't walk over to a chair, so the desk would have to do.

"Fine," she snapped finally. "Let's call her now, before I get any angrier at you. Depending on what she tells me, I may have to make preparations for the spellwork required. The sooner we start this, the sooner we let loose the spells of war."

"I thought that quote was supposed to be *let loose the dogs of war.*" He thawed out enough to quirk one side of his mouth into a tiny grin.

"Dogs. Spells. Whatever. It works for me. My spells have teeth when I want them to." She smiled a false smile. "Just you remember that, Mr. Mayor."

That wiped the small grin from his face. One part of her was sad to see it go. Another part wanted to slap him for being such a beast to her. So they hadn't told the complete truth, but then again, neither had the residents of Grizzly Cove. They were pretending to be a group of human artists, for goodness' sake. Although, the art she'd seen in the galleries in town was very pretty. Maybe they really were artists, but John definitely had warrior stamped all over his impatient, very fit, handsome bod.

Urse had always figured there would be a few shifters in a place as wild as this. That was to be expected. Shifters lived among humans all over the world. She'd thought nothing of the few townsfolk she'd met on her one and only scouting trip to the area. They'd been shifters. Big deal. She figured the rest of the town was human, and that was good enough for her.

Only upon moving up here lock, stock and barrel had they realized that there were only three—*THREE*—humans in town. The three Baker sisters, and they were all in the process of marrying shifters, so they had to be in on the secret already.

There really was no solution to the problem. The shifters probably couldn't tell they were *strega*, and therefore weren't obliged to tell people they thought were clueless humans about their true nature. By the same token, the Ricoletti sisters had thought this was a *normal* town, with just a higher-than-average number of shifters because of the ruggedness of the locale. That was a logical conclusion to have drawn on such short acquaintance with the place, so they'd done nothing wrong in not telling anyone about their powers.

Only after they'd gotten here and realized where they'd ended up...well...that was when Urse should have overruled Mellie and sought out the mayor to come clean. But she'd been enjoying being in Grizzly Cove. The place was beautiful. The cove was so peaceful… Except for the little sea monster problem that had cropped up today.

Which she was going to do something about.

Steeling her resolve, she reached for the phone. "I'm calling Nonna. You already have her number down as our emergency contact, so I don't mind inputting it into your phone system. Nonna is a better witch than me and Mellie put together, so if any of you go after her, you're going to regret it," she warned as she dialed.

John looked affronted. "What in the world do you take me for? I don't go after grannies with intent to kill. Not unless they're grannies who work for the *Venifucus*. Yours doesn't, does she?" He was almost shouting at her.

Urse made the sign of the cross when he said the V word. It was an old habit from growing up with a very Catholic Nonna. "Don't you dare say that about my Nonna!"

"I didn't say she was one of them," he insisted. "I said she only had to worry about us if she was."

"Well, she's not!" Say anything you like about Urse herself, but don't attack her Nonna. That's when the claws came out.

She punched in the final number, and the phone started to ring. She was shaking, she was so worked up.

"How do you put this thing on speaker?" she grudgingly asked John, practically slamming the phone back onto the desk. He came over and punched a button, and then, the electronic ring tone sounded through the office.

She glared at him while it rang, and then finally, on the fifth ring, the line was picked up.

"Hello?" Nonna's heavily accented voice came over the speaker.

"Nonna, it's me, Urse. I'm in the Grizzly Cove town hall with the mayor, John Marshall, and you're on speaker, okay?" She tried to speak clearly. Nonna's hearing wasn't as good as it used to be.

"Oh! You're with Johnny," Nonna replied, sounding for all the world as if she knew the mayor already, though Urse was pretty sure she'd never laid eyes on him in her life. "Good. So. You have a problem up there, *sì*?"

"Nonna…" Urse wasn't sure how to tackle this. Nonna often knew more than she should. Then again, she was a powerful and very old *strega*. Who knew what sorts of gifts she really had? Nonna hadn't revealed everything to her granddaughters. Not yet. "I was attacked today…"

"By the leviathan," Nonna said knowingly.

"I beg your pardon, ma'am," John broke in, "but how could you know that?"

"Just as I saw your face, Johnny, I saw the creature that haunts your coast. It is why I sent my granddaughters to you," came Nonna's mysterious reply.

"You saw this?" Urse was shocked. Nonna had occasional bouts of clairvoyance. It wasn't her greatest gift, but when the visions came, they were strong and eerily accurate.

"*Sì.* You cannot defeat the leviathan yourselves. Neither you nor your sister. But you can protect those innocent people on the land…and some of those in the sea. Your spells will help the land dwellers, but your sister must seek a way to assist the sea creatures. All creatures who serve the Light suffer when the leviathan is near." Nonna paused, and Urse met John's gaze. She was glad he looked as stunned as she felt. "Three will come to fight the leviathan. They will each play their role, but it will be the unexpected that finally banishes the creature from our realm again. Watch for them. They will come when the time is right, and not before."

"Nonna. Did you just give him a prophecy?" Urse could hardly believe it. She knew for a fact that her grandmother didn't just hand out prophecies lightly. Usually, it involved all sorts of rigmarole—probably because it didn't happen often.

"I did," her grandmother confirmed. "And you can just lift your jaw up off the floor, Ursula. Things have changed in the world. Dark times are coming. We must all band together to help one another at such times. This feuding and distrust between our races must end, or else we're all doomed."

Urse gulped. "Doomed?"

Now, she knew her granny had always had a bit of a dramatic flair, but this was going above and beyond. Never before had she said anything so dire.

"*Si, figlia mia*, doomed. It is no less than the truth."

"Wow." Urse slumped where she was sitting. She'd never heard anything like that from her grandmother before. This was bad. Really bad.

"*Si*. Now you understand." Her grandmother paused before continuing to speak in her heavily-accented English. "Now listen well. You will need all your skill and strength to do what must be done. And you must do it soon. Prepare tonight for the breaking dawn ceremony of Light. You must do this tomorrow. Continue the day after, at noon, and the following day at sunset. You will be at your strongest when the Light shines upon you. Unfortunately, it is winter now, and the days are short, but there is still hope, for the moon will be at its fullest in four days' time. You must conclude your part in protecting the town with a full moon ceremony on that last night. It would be best if you can get some of those brave bears to watch over you while you work, and perhaps lend some of their strength, if they are willing, to enhance your wards."

"Oh, I don't think it'll be any problem to get at least one of them to watch my back. The mayor has already informed me that he's not willing to let me do magic without his supervision." Urse was still annoyed by the mayor's insistence.

"*Si*. That is good. You will need the Alpha bear behind you if this is going to work. He will stand for all his people during the daytime ceremonies, but at night, it would be best to have a small gathering in a sacred place, as close to the beach as you dare. I saw..." Nonna trailed off, uncharacteristically uncertain. "There was a circle of stones. Not big standing stones, but something that looked more natural, but wasn't. A sacred circle, hidden in plain sight. On a rocky point where sea spray can reach, but not consume— at least not normally. You must be careful. It is a dangerous

36

place that calls to good and evil alike. You can use this power for good. The evil thing will seek its power to devour it. It will attack, but you must stand strong. You *all* must stand strong. Or you all fail."

"Fail?" Urse croaked. Failure in magical circles often equaled death.

"We will not fail, ma'am. Not with my town on the line. Not with my people holding the line. You should know that most of us are retired soldiers," John revealed, surprising Urse. "We never run from a fight."

"Seems I wasn't the only one keeping secrets," Urse muttered. "Do you know the place Nonna is talking about?"

John looked grim as he nodded. "I know it. It's not an easy hike, and it'll be dangerous at night."

"But you must go there," Nonna said stridently through the phone. "It is the only way to fully protect your land-based shifters from the leviathan. It is the only place that can channel enough power. Ursula, make him understand. Teach him about our ways, if you must, to convince him."

John's eyebrows rose, right along with Urse's. Never had her Nonna instructed her to divulge family secrets to a non-mage before. This was serious.

"Are you sure?" Urse double-checked.

"Positive. It is the only way," her grandmother said at once.

"Well, if you say so," Urse agreed somewhat reluctantly. This was big. Bigger than she'd even imagined.

"And get Amelia to call me tomorrow morning. I have instructions for her as well, though it is not yet time for her to participate," Nonna ordered quickly. "Now, you have preparations to make. I send all my love to you, Ursula, and to you, Johnny. If all goes well, we will meet one day, and I will see your handsome face in person."

John's lips quirked up in a crooked smile. "Yes, ma'am. I look forward to it. Thank you for your help."

"All of us who serve the Light must help each other now. I will pray for you, *figlio mio*, and all of the people you protect and serve."

Urse was surprised by her grandmother's warm tone for the man who had so easily gotten under Urse's skin with his attitude about magic—or more specifically, his distrust of her now that he knew she was a *strega*.

"*Ciao, Nonna. Ti voglio molto bene.* I'll call you tomorrow and let you know how the dawn ceremony goes."

"See that you do," Nonna said with mock sternness.

She gave Urse a few more words of caution and encouragement before she let the call end with a long-distance blessing that called on the Mother of All and a few of her favorite saints thrown in for good measure. Nonna had a strange way of looking at the two religions the *strega* had blended together, but she made it work. Somehow.

Silence fell in the front office of town hall for a moment after the call ended. Urse had punched the button to end the call, then sat back, nonplussed. So much had happened in such a short time. When she'd risen this morning, she hadn't expected all this excitement. And now she had a mission—and a heck of a lot of magic to do over the next four days.

She looked up to find John staring at her. She did her best not to fidget under his warm chocolate gaze, remembering belatedly that she still wasn't wearing any makeup and she was probably a mess from both the dust in the store and her headlong flight across the sand.

"Sounds like we've got our work cut out for us. Tell me what you need from me, Ms. Ricoletti, and I'll see that you have it. Within reason, of course."

"Don't worry. I won't be asking you to find eye of newt or anything like that," she quipped, hopping down from her perch on the desk. "Though I can't vouch for my sister on that score." She tested out her knees to find that they were much more stable. Talking to Nonna had helped calm the last of her reaction high. Nonna had given her a plan...and marching orders. There was work to do. "Right now, I have to get back home. There are a few things I need to gather and prepare before dawn tomorrow. You'll need to do a few things too."

"Like what?" he asked, a bit of wariness entering his gaze.

"Nothing too hard, mayor. First, you'll need to take a shower before you join me. Just water. No soap. No fragrances or anything fancy. Just the water and you, to wash you clean of the night and prepare your spirit for the work at hand. Then you have to dress in natural fibers. You own jeans, right? Cotton? And maybe a cotton shirt or wool pullover? Natural colors are best, if you can manage that. Browns, greens, black, white. You get the idea. Also, don't eat before you meet up with me. The fasting period of the night will break with the dawn, and after I cast the wards, we can have breakfast. Not before. No casting on a full stomach for me, or for those observing. We'll need a lantern or other source of open flame. I have a little brazier we can use, but we might need a windbreak depending on where we set up and weather conditions."

John frowned. This sounded a lot more complicated than he'd thought it would be.

"Where do you want to start? Geographically," he clarified when she just blinked at him.

"Oh. Yeah. I think we should start at the apex of the cove. Right across the street from the bakery. That's pretty much the center of town, right?" John nodded. "Where is the circle of stones Nonna mentioned?"

John stepped over to the wall, where an artist's rendering of the cove hung. Some of Tom's finest work, John thought, and handy for this discussion.

"The stone circle is at the point," he said, directing her to the southern point where the ocean was separated from the cove by a small triangle of land that jutted out into the sea. The northern point was a little less pronounced, but shaped somewhat the same. Between the two points was the mouth of the bay that formed Grizzly Cove.

"Hmm." Ursula walked over to stand next to him, examining the painting. "That changes things a bit. We have four days and four ceremonies. We should spread them out in the most sensible pattern. I wanted to start here in town, but since we'll be ending at the southern point, we'll have to readjust a bit." She seemed to ponder the problem a moment before nodding. "Okay. This is what we'll do. We'll start here." She pointed to the northern edge of the town. "I'll be facing east as the sun rises, but turn west when it shines over my shoulders. The first part of the ceremony will be the most dangerous. We need to start as close to dawn as we dare, without missing the critical moment."

"Can we start away from the beach and walk closer after the sun rises?" John asked, considering the tactical aspects of what she planned to do. She looked at him with what seemed like surprise before nodding slowly.

"That might possibly work, if I cast my circle on the large side. It would protect more of the town as I work too. I'll need a lot of salt. Can you rally your troops and get them to donate all their salt to the cause? Sea salt is better, but I'll take any ol' table salt too. The more, the better."

"How about rock salt? We have a stock of that to de-ice the roads."

"That could work. We'll need to start early so I can cast a big enough circle, and we could probably use a few guards to make sure nobody messes with it. Just in town though. I don't want anybody on the beach, in the danger zone."

"I'll get Brody and Zak and a few of the others," John promised, already thinking ahead, planning the mission. It was one of the strangest ops he'd ever planned, that was for sure, but it might just be one of the most important—if it would help keep his people safe.

CHAPTER FOUR

They kept working on the plan for about an hour. Eventually, Brody came back, and John pulled him in to help keep track of what they would need, laying out the problem in impressively few words. John really knew how to boil things down to the basics, and that was something Urse could respect.

He'd even sent someone over to the bookstore to keep Mellie company, though Urse didn't quite know how to feel about that. Was the man sent to keep her safe or to keep the town safe from the mad *strega* on the loose? Was the guy intended to be a companion or a jailer?

Urse figured she wouldn't find out 'til she got back to the store, and she couldn't do anything about it at the moment. John probably wouldn't even consider starting to trust her again until she proved herself in some way. Maybe after he saw her in action tomorrow at dawn, doing her all—and giving all her energy—to safeguard the town and its people. Maybe that would help win back his regard.

She found it mattered. A lot. And that was weird. It had been a long time since a man's opinion of her had mattered quite this much to Urse. Not since Tony Albernoni had broken her heart in high school when she'd started acting weird because her power had been coming to life and she hadn't known how to handle it back then.

Since then, in fact, she'd steered mostly clear of human men. There was the occasional passing warlock, but those guys weren't really interested in long-term commitments with someone of her level of power. Her bloodlines were too diluted with the shifter blood—even as far back as it went— to interest any of the really powerful mages.

When it came down to it, the magical community was filled with snobs. Every last one of them.

Only among the *strega* did she and Mellie fit in. A sisterhood that traced its roots back to Italy and a small group of women who kept the magic alive in their families and their descendants. They had welcomed her, regardless of the shifter blood that others said *tainted* their line. Among *strega*, the Ricoletti name was well respected for its past deeds and unwavering service to the Light.

That seemed to count among shifters as well, which Urse liked. They weren't snobs. At least not that she'd seen since moving here. They were good, honest, sometimes irreverent people who seemed to judge people on their actions.

Which was why she had a lot to prove to John tomorrow morning. She'd hidden the truth from him. She didn't think it qualified as an outright lie, but it was something that definitely stood between them now. And more and more, she realized she didn't like the distance between herself and the hunky mayor.

No, she liked John a little too much to tolerate his suspicion. She wanted it gone. And the only way she thought she could accomplish that feat was to prove to him that she meant no harm to anyone. She just wanted to coexist and make friends. That's all. Nothing sinister or covert.

There would be no more hiding what she was. She was *strega,* and she was proud. And damn it all—she even had a bit of bear shifter blood in her ancestry, which should count for something among these people. It sure as heck had made her life difficult among magic users, who saw it as a major flaw.

"I think we've got just about every angle covered, right?" John said, breaking into her thoughts. "Unless you have something else to tell me?"

And there it was. He totally didn't trust her.

"No, John." She bit her lip and prayed for patience. "I've told you everything you can expect tomorrow. The only things I've left out are the things I can't predict. Such as, how the creature is going to react, and what effect my spells will ultimately have."

John met her gaze and leaned back in his chair. They'd moved into his office to do their planning. It was just them, with John using his phone a lot to contact various people as the plan developed.

"One thing any old soldier will tell you is that the mission plan seldom survives the first engagement. But don't worry. We're experienced at this sort of thing. Well, maybe not dealing with sea monsters, in particular, but with unpredictable enemies and less-than-ideal circumstances. My men and I know what to do, and more than that, we'll have your back, Ursula."

She felt the impact of his statement down to her bones. Just like that, she felt more solid about what they were planning to do tomorrow. All the while they'd been talking about it, she'd felt very exposed by the plan. She was going to be the focal point, after all. The only magic user, surrounded by shifters who may or may not care if she lived or died. At least, that's what she'd thought until about two seconds ago.

Urse saw the seriousness in his gaze, and she felt the pull of his words and his intentions. He was going to protect her to the best of his ability. Suddenly, she felt warm. Like the sun had come out on a rainy Pacific Northwest winter day.

"Thank you for that, John," she replied quietly, with the utmost sincerity. "It makes me feel a lot better to know that I won't be all alone, even if I am the only one wielding magic tomorrow." She thought about that for a moment. "Well, besides the leviathan."

And just like that, the nerves were back. She forced them

down. She wouldn't show weakness. Not now. Not ever.

"I'm still not clear on why your sister can't help," John said, standing as she did the same.

"Because her kind of magic is quite different and distinct from my own. Plus, Nonna said she was going to be busy brewing potions to purify the water, when the time comes. I'm the one who's supposed to deal with the land." She stretched a bit, feeling a tiny bit of soreness from her headlong run earlier. "And Nonna's never wrong about who does what. We learned that early on when we were learning our craft from her. Any time we switched up tasks she had set for us, we screwed up royally. Nonna knows our skills almost better than we do ourselves. Trust me, John. She's been at this for a very long time. Nobody argues with Nonna." She smiled as she turned toward the door to his office.

"She sounds like a formidable woman," he said kindly, which made her look up at his handsome face. He was smiling that crooked grin of his that was fast becoming her favorite of his many expressions. Probably because it was so rare.

"If she'd ever been in an army, she'd be a four-star general," Urse quipped.

"I bet..." his voice dropped to an intimate level as they stood only a few feet apart by the door, "...you take after her."

Urse couldn't hold back her laughter. "Oh, man." She continued to chuckle as she moved through the doorway into the hall. "I have to admit, the older I get the more I see the signs." She went down the hall, toward the front reception area of the new town hall building. "Mellie takes more after our mom, whereas I greatly fear I'm turning into my grandmother."

Urse found herself enjoying the light rumble of his laughter as they entered the open reception area. She turned slightly, expecting him to say goodbye and send her on her way, but he surprised her by walking past her to open the door and gesture for her to precede him.

"I hope you don't mind if I walk you home. With everything that's happened today, I want to make sure you get there safely," he said, but she immediately became suspicious.

"Is this just a friendly gesture, or is it because you want me watched at all times?" Her resentment came through her tone, and she didn't really care if he noticed.

"For now, just call it a friendly protective action. Honey, you almost bought it earlier today. I don't want anything else happening to you before we do the deed tomorrow morning."

Okay. First, he'd called her honey. After that little endearment slapped her upside the head with an unexpectedly erotic velvet caress, he'd said the words *do the deed*, and her mind had gone straight to the sex place. With him. The mayor of freaking Bear City, USA.

Okay, it wasn't called that. Only in her mind, maybe. But it was definitely the shifter-iest place she'd ever been in her life. And every single one of them she'd seen had tasted of bear to her magical senses.

Most mages couldn't differentiate between animals, but she had shifter blood, so she had a little edge. And her shifter blood was bear, so she recognized her own even better than the others.

And bears loved honey. And he'd just called her honey. Something he loved...

Oh, get a grip, Urse!

"Well, uh..." Much to her chagrin, she had to clear her throat before she could actually speak. "That's mighty neighborly of you."

Dull, Urse. Way to go.

But he hadn't been talking about having sex with her. No matter where her wayward thoughts had taken her. He'd been talking about her doing magic while he did his best—with his team of bear shifter commandos around him—to protect her from a giant freaking sea monster that wanted her blood...and her magic.

So dull was good. She was fairly certain he wasn't thinking about sex and her in the same universe. Why such thoughts were suddenly popping into her mind was beyond her. Except maybe it was that kind of thing where when you have a near-death experience, suddenly you want to celebrate life by grabbing the nearest hot guy and boinking like bunnies? Maybe?

Although...Urse had been in some pretty tight spots from time to time as she learned her craft. She'd come closer to dying than she was comfortable admitting a time or two. And she hadn't felt like jumping the nearest stranger and doing him 'til the sun rose.

So what had changed? Why now? Why *him*?

They walked down Main Street side by side. It was only a short distance from the town hall, which was on one end of the small strip that was considered the center of town, to the bookstore, which was just past the bakery, which was at the mid-point.

"Do you have enough provisions in your apartment or do you want to stop at the bakery and get something for dinner?" he asked solicitously as they walked along.

"I set up a pan of lasagna this morning. Mellie's probably cooked it by now. There's plenty, if you want to join us."

Holy crap. Did she just invite John to dinner? Where the hell had that come from?

Probably from the same instinct that had sent her mind straight to the sex place at the least provocation.

"Real Italian lasagna?" John actually smiled at her, and her heart went pitter-pat without her permission. "How could I refuse?"

Sweet Mother in heaven, he's going to come to dinner. Her inner teenager stood up and cheered, then squealed with excitement. *Yeah, right. Real mature, Urse.*

They made it to the bookstore without mishap, only to find that Mellie had already invited the guy John had sent over to keep her company to join them for lasagna too. Seemed like little sis wanted to get to know more about the big Russian named Peter Zilakov.

Urse was glad she'd made the big pan full of lasagna. They'd intended to freeze what they didn't eat, but with two big strapping bear shifters joining them, there weren't going to be any leftovers. That was okay. Urse liked cooking. She could always make more.

Peter owned the butcher shop. It was an old-fashioned establishment that catered to eclectic tastes. Urse had been able to get veal and mutton in addition to bison, regular pork, beef, and poultry. He also had some more specialized meats always in stock, such as alligator, ostrich and even rattlesnake. He apparently ordered some of the more exotic meats in, but he was also a hunter who would sell the wild things he and some of the others in town hunted.

Urse enjoyed his dinner conversation and the camaraderie between him and John. It was clear Peter respected John, but they were easy in each other's presence in a way Urse hadn't expected. She figured the Alpha of the Clan would be the grand poobah or something, but John didn't really stand on ceremony with his men from what Urse had seen.

Peter was telling them about how he was going to have to expand his business a bit when the new restaurant finally opened. Construction had just started next to the bakery, and the restaurant was going to be run by the current deputy, Zak, who was going to work part-time for the sheriff after his business opened. Which meant there might be an opening for another deputy when the time came.

"So who are you looking at to help the sheriff?" Urse asked John. "The town council must have some ideas."

"Really, anybody could do it," Peter put in, his faint Russian accent charming. "Most of the core group is ex-military. We all have the right kind of experience."

"Yeah, but who wants it?" John asked rhetorically. "A lot of us are sick of peacekeeping. Done too much of it in every crappy corner of the world."

"I could help out at night, maybe," Peter offered. "I close the shop at three in the afternoon. After that, I'm mostly free."

"That could work," John said, considering. "Talk to Brody about it. I think Zak is going to work mornings for the town, then spend his nights at the restaurant."

"When will it be finished?" Mellie asked.

"Depends on the weather, really," John answered. "We get a mild winter, it could be done quicker than we think, but if we keep having other troubles—magical ones—then it might never get finished."

That caused a bit of a lull, and Urse figured, since he brought it up, they might as well talk about it. John wouldn't have mentioned it in front of Peter if he didn't trust the man.

"Mel, I didn't really get a chance to tell you about talking to Nonna today," Urse began, but her sister waved her down.

"She called me right after she hung up with you," Mellie said. Urse probably shouldn't have been surprised. Nonna was always thorough, and she probably had a few words of advice she'd wanted to give directly to Mel. "She wants you to do your thing first, then I'm going to follow up with some pretty intricate potion work that could take a while. I might be ready by next month's full moon, but that'd be pushing it. More likely, it'll be a bit after that."

"So you time to prepare, and I have to jump in head-first tomorrow? Damn." Urse sipped the red wine they'd served with the dinner as they sat around, finishing the last of their meal.

Mellie laughed at her. Urse stuck her tongue out at her sister. Childish, but they loved each other. They just had a funny way of showing it sometimes.

"Nonna doesn't even want me to be your backup tomorrow. She made me promise to stay home." Mellie looked upset by that. "I'm sorry, Urse."

"It is what it is. Don't worry. John here is going to be my backup." Urse gestured toward the mayor with her glass.

"I won't let anything happen to her," he said solemnly, directly to Mellie.

"See that you don't," Mellie replied, uncharacteristically

fierce.

John nodded, uninsulted.

Urse turned to Peter, wanting to change the subject. "So, Peter, you don't seem too upset by the whole *strega* thing. What gives?"

Peter shrugged. "I'm Russian. Things are different in the old country. The countries that have been around more than a piddling two hundred years have seen magic before. My own *babushka* used to seek out the *ved'ma* in the small village near where we lived when she needed potions and advice on magical issues." Peter seemed to think back, clearly touched by thoughts of his past. "My *babushka*—you know this word, right? It means grandmother. She was the best."

"To grandmothers," Mellie said, raising her glass, proposing a toast. "What would we have become without them?"

Peter smiled and they drank the toast. "I shudder to think what would have become of me without my *babushka*."

"Is she still around?" Mellie asked quietly.

"Yes," Peter replied with a wide smile. "In fact, she is coming to visit. If she likes the town, she may stay. There is little keeping her in Russia now, and I would like to have her closer, but I gave up the motherland and will not go back for many years, if ever."

Urse sensed a story there, but it was clear Peter didn't want to go into detail.

"I wonder what your *babushka* will make of all us American bears?" John said, grinning.

"That, we will have to see for ourselves, but I think she's going to enjoy this place and its people. She's a very forward-thinking woman and still in good health, despite her age," Peter said with obvious joy.

"You shifters live a lot longer than regular folk, don't you?" Urse asked.

"Most of us get a few centuries if we're lucky," John confirmed. "How old is your granny, Pete? Two-fifty? Two-sixty?"

"About that, but she won't tell us the exact date." Peter laughed. "She only admits to being born during the reign of Peter the Great. He reigned from 1672 to 1725."

Urse was stunned, though the two shifters seemed to take it in stride.

"Then she was around during the Russian revolution?" Urse said, a bit of awe creeping into her tone.

"Oh, yes. But she was not a big fan of the Soviets. Neither was I, in fact, though I started my career as a soldier under the old system. Over time, as communism fell, things changed, and I had to keep moving to outrun the records that would have betrayed my true age to the wrong people in the government. Eventually, I ended up under John's command, and the rest, as they say, is history."

"I get the feeling this town is out of the norm," Mellie put in, taking the conversation in a different direction. "Don't bears usually like to roam alone?"

"It's all a big social experiment," Peter agreed, nodding to John. "We follow the Alpha, though we're not as fanatical about it as some other species. Wolves, for example, will do just about anything the top dog tells them with blind faith. Bears are a little more discerning." Both John and Peter chuckled.

"Which is why you have a town council," Urse realized aloud. "You're the Alpha bear, but you listen to your people more, right?"

"That's about the size of it," John admitted freely. "I may be the most Alpha of the guys, but I'm not a tyrant."

"To the benevolent despot." Peter raised his glass, smiling broadly. They all chuckled, but drank to the toast.

The men took their leave not long after, Peter heading out first, waving goodbye casually, though his gaze seemed to linger just a bit on Mellie. Or maybe that was just Urse's imagination.

After Peter was gone, Mellie began cleaning up, leaving Urse to see John out. She walked with him to the door, but he paused, speaking to her in a low, almost intimate tone.

"I'll be by to get you an hour before dawn. Will that give you enough time to set up?" he asked.

"That's enough," she said, swallowing hard, feeling a few nerves starting to jangle as time counted down to when she would need to act.

"Don't go outside without me," he cautioned. "Wait for me to come. I promise I'll be here. You have my cell number, right?"

She nodded. "You gave it to me when we first arrived. It's programmed into my phone, though I didn't think I'd ever really need it."

"You feel free to use it any time, day or night. I mean that, Ursula, okay?"

Again, she nodded. "Thanks." Nerves were starting to get to her a bit now. His serious tone made it hard to forget that, in just a few hours, she would be facing off against that awful creature again.

But this time, she knew what she was up against. Mostly. She wasn't sure how strong it was, or how it would test her, but at least she knew of its existence now and was prepared to fight back. That was something, right?

"Hey…" John took both of her hands in his, and it was then she realized her hands were trembling, just the tiniest bit. "It's gonna be okay. I'll be right there with you. I won't let anything bad happen. I promise."

"How can you promise something like that? Did you see the size of that thing?" She remembered her headlong flight earlier that afternoon and looking back to see the gigantic scale of the creature that literally made the earth shake with its anger.

"Aw, hell. Come here."

He pulled her into his arms, and she went gladly, the fear taking over for just a few short moments. She needed to get over this. She needed to be strong. Later. She had a few precious hours before she had to be strong and face that freaking monster again.

"Ssh," he soothed her, rubbing one hand over the back of her head, stroking her hair and then down her back, only to start over again. The repetitive motion went a long way toward calming her. "It'll be okay. I promise."

"How can you say that, John?" She pulled back slightly to look at him. "We're going up against something not even of this realm. I've never done anything like this before. I have no idea if I'm even ready to wield that kind of magic."

"Your grandmother thinks you're ready," he reminded her. "That's got to count for something, right? I get the impression she wouldn't send you against this thing, if she didn't think you could handle it. Wouldn't she be calling for the cavalry right about now?"

Urse thought about that. "You know…" She smiled up at him. "I never thought of that. You're right."

And just like that, her panic attack was no more. *Damn.* The Alpha bear was magic. The past few minutes proved that to her beyond the shadow of a doubt.

His arms were still around her, but she didn't really want him to let her go. No, it was incredibly comfortable where she was, and oddly enough, she felt safe with him, in ways she had never really felt before. Something about this big, strong Alpha bear made her want to snuggle up against him and just…stay there a while. A good long while.

And more. Though she didn't think she was ready to examine those somewhat scandalous feelings just yet.

But apparently he was.

Urse saw his kiss coming a mile away, but she didn't move. She didn't dare breathe. She suddenly wanted his lips on hers more than she'd ever wanted anything in her life.

He'd broadcast his intentions, and she'd all but given him the green light. In fact, the light was blinking green in Morse code saying, *take me now, big guy.*

And then, he did.

His lips touched hers, and everything changed. Time slowed. The earth seemed to stop altogether, for just that moment. His lips were warm and tender, then harder, more demanding. Asking her to comply instead of ordering her compliance. She liked that. She liked everything she had learned about him. About the way he ruled his men and this town, and now, about the way he kissed.

Like a dream. That's what it was. He kissed like the best dream she'd ever had.

It was all over far too quickly. His lips lifted away, but his gaze tracked hers, his mouth smiling as she felt the lethargy of passion lifting away like fog burning off in the morning.

Damn. He was potent. She felt drugged. And all that from just a kiss.

"I'll see you in a few hours," he said, his voice rumbling low now, making her belly clench.

Would he talk that way in the bedroom after they'd made love? Wouldn't she like to know?

CHAPTER FIVE

As promised, John was back in the hour before dawn. He was showered, his golden brown hair still glistening wet in the sexiest way, and he looked good enough to eat. But that was a thought Urse kept carefully to herself.

They went out into the darkness with great caution. Armed men were all around, forming a cordon as she started casting the circle. It would have to be a big circle to do the trick. She started at one side and worked her way around. She'd have to be careful when they neared the beach. She'd do that bit, closest to the water, as fast as possible. Just in case.

"It would be best to keep your men outside the circle, and away from the water," she said to John in a low voice as she worked.

He was right next to her, helping her. This first part of the process was mostly mechanical. She'd said a blessing over the big bag of rock salt they'd procured for her and began to lay the thin line of salt that would form the circle. The men were cognizant enough to keep clear of the line, once she'd laid it.

It was slow work because this circle was going to be the biggest she'd ever cast. But once it was complete, it would—hopefully—shield her from whatever the leviathan was going to throw at her. The men outside though... She had to impress upon them just how dangerous this could be.

"The guys and I discussed this, but we don't really know what to expect, right?" John said. He was holding the fifty-pound sack of salt for her as they made their way around the perimeter, laying out the circle a few feet at a time.

"The minute this circle closes, expect all hell to break loose," she told him, speaking loud enough for the men around them to hear. "You men should stay behind the circle. Theoretically, anything inside—meaning me—should be okay."

"And me," John put in, his voice a deep rumble next to her. "I'm staying in here with you, if that won't put you in more danger."

She shook her head, totally surprised by his intention to stay with her.

"Once the circle is closed, it should be self-sustaining unless someone or something breaks it. You can stay with me, but John…" She paused a moment to touch his arm. "You really shouldn't. This will be the focal point for the beast's wrath. I'll be protected from its magical attacks—in theory—inside the circle, but I'll also be launching magic of my own outward. That's the nature of the circle I'm casting here. It keeps magical things out but allows my magic to cross the barrier. There may be a bit of a buildup in here before I launch. It could get uncomfortable."

"I have quite a bit of magic of my own, Ursula. Bears are among the most magical of all werecreatures. I'll help you if I can. It's my home. The whole town was my idea. I should bear some of the burden of protecting it. This shouldn't be all on you."

Once again surprised by his gentle tone and deep thoughts, she thought about how she could make this work. And then, the men on the outside of the line she'd been drawing with salt had their spokesman come over.

"We've been listening in," Sheriff Brody said in that urgent soldier voice of his. "We can do our part outside too, ma'am."

"What?" She honestly hadn't expected this. Since last night, she'd been so worried that she'd be all on her own, but here were allies. Strong allies, if she wasn't much mistaken.

"None of us are proper mages, but we're experienced with the use of magical barriers and fortifications. We've used them in the field a few times, when no humans were around to see what we were doing." Brody winked at her while he and John chuckled.

Why were they laughing? Didn't they know they were about to face down a giant fucking sea serpent?

"Who *are* you people?" She heard the words come out of her mouth, too late to stop them.

Now they were all laughing.

"Oh, honey," John said between chuckles. "You knew a lot of us were soldiers, right? I guess you didn't realize that up 'til very recently we were all part of one of Uncle Sam's elite Special Forces teams. We're used to this kind of thing."

"Well…" Brody put in from the other side of the salt line. "Maybe not this exact sort of thing, but we're used to danger and stopping bad guys. It's actually kind of nice to be back in the real world again, doing stuff that matters."

She couldn't really argue with that. This mattered. This was a battle for their hometown. What could be more important than the fight of good against evil?

"I didn't realize…" she whispered, trying to think how best to use their abilities. "This isn't a traditional fight. You can't beat this thing. It can't be killed in this realm."

"Yeah, John told us," Brody said. "We've got specialized help coming—eventually—but until they can get here, we're it, so we'd better make this good."

Until a few minutes ago, she'd thought she was *it*, as the sheriff had put it. But this could work. In fact, this could *really* work.

"I didn't realize I was going to have help," she told them honestly as she resumed pouring the salt line. They had to get the circle cast before dawn, or this would all be for naught. "Do you guys want to come inside the circle with me?"

"Better not," Brody said after looking at John for a moment. "We're better if we're mobile. The Alpha will watch your back from inside. We'll back you up from outside."

"Okay, but I don't want any of you down by the water. You need to stay out of physical reach of the creature, and those tentacles are *freaking* long." She shuddered as she remembered the day before. "Don't go any closer than halfway down the circle. And whatever you do, *do not* touch the salt. If the circle breaks, I'm toast."

"So we guard the perimeter," Brody agreed, nodding. "We can also distract the creature with our magic while you work yours."

"I'll be channeling the energy of the sunrise and the blessings of the Goddess to protect this section of the cove. If you can distract the leviathan without putting yourselves in too much danger, it would be a big help. You'll probably be able to see the Light of dawn gather inside the circle before I release it. The leviathan shouldn't be able to see it until the last moment, but since you're the good guys, you might be able to see the glow of it. That's the critical point. I'll need time to gather it and release it at its zenith, when the dawn breaks."

"Roger that," Brody said. "I'll brief the team. Lady be with you both."

"You too, sheriff," she said as she realized they were nearing the tricky part of the beach.

"Keep watch now," John directed Brody. "We're going to go fast over this section, and when we hit the point where we started, I expect things will start happening fast, right?"

"Exactly right," she confirmed. "It's almost show time, but if it's close, it could strike any time before I get the circle closed. Everybody stay sharp."

Brody nodded and walked carefully off, already talking into the tiny radio clipped to his ear. His eyes scanned the pre-dawn darkness of the cove, and everyone seemed to come to an alert posture.

She turned to John. "I'm going to move fast now. I'm

going right in front of that big rock there. I think that'll get me close enough to do the job. Are you ready?"

John touched her shoulder, placing a surprising kiss on her forehead that felt like both a benediction and a caress.

"I'm with you. Let's do this."

Urse moved as fast as she could past the shoreline, casting the salt as neatly and quickly as she could to form the circle. When she reached the point where she had started, she took a deep breath, spoke a word of high magic, and laid the final grains.

With a whoosh of power audible only to those who could actually hear magic, the protection slammed into place. And then, as predicted, all hell broke loose.

The water churned. Tentacles appearing at random points all over the cove.

Sweet Mother of All! The leviathan was even bigger than she'd imagined. For a breathless moment, Urse stood motionless, taking it all in. And for just that moment, she almost lost her nerve.

"Take it easy," John said, his deep voice rumbling near her ear. "We've got this."

Shutting her eyes and taking a deep breath to center herself, Urse silently thanked the Lady that John had decided to put himself on the line, to be by her side. His strength, and the conviction that came through his words, renewed her courage.

She reached for his hand, squeezing it in thanks even as a gentle calm came over her. That was John's magic, brushing against hers.

Trapped inside the protection of her circle, she could feel the gentle thrum of his power—vast, timeless and so very Alpha. How had she missed it before?

But that was a thought for later. Right now, she had a sea monster to fight.

Urse strode into the center of her circle and turned her back on the thrashing in the cove. The leviathan was getting closer, testing the strength of her wards. Urse's goal was to gather as much of the power and magic of sunrise into her circle before she could release it against the creature. She would use the magic of the earth, and the Light, to lay the strongest protections possible on the cove. If this worked, within the hour, at least part of the cove would be a no-go zone for anything with evil intent.

She raised her hands, facing the mountains in the east, over which the sun would rise, and began to chant. She alternated the chanting with spoken prayers to the Lady, and she could feel the power begin to coalesce around her, filling the circle with pure magic.

Soon, the sun would rise, and the power would be at its apex. That would be her moment to strike.

John felt the most incredible energy gathering around them. He had a front row seat to the most amazing magic show he'd ever seen. And that was saying something.

Bears were among the most magical of shifters. They got used to seeing a lot of strange things. As leader of the Alpha Team, John had seen, and done, a lot more than most. But this was something new in his experience. Something good and pure.

Something he knew he could help with.

John stood back to back with Ursula. She faced the mountains. He faced the writhing waters of the cove, alive with not just the giant leviathan, but what looked like an army of its offspring.

He added his own silent prayers to the ones Ursula was speaking, and possibly for the first time in his life, he felt magic in a new way. Shifter magic was of the earth, and of the Mother Goddess. Human magic had a different flavor. But Ursula's magic was somewhere in between. Close to his own, with a distinct tinge of bear—probably from the shifter way back in her bloodline—but unique in its own right.

The human magic John had witnessed in the past called upon the Goddess as well, but this *strega* magic called much more directly upon Her Light. It was hard to describe, but it

BIANCA D'ARC

felt like Ursula's magic was closer to the core. Closer to the Mother of All in some indefinable way. John was gaining a new understanding of the slight variations that made each race's magic a little different.

Urusla's chant ended while she seemed to take a moment to regroup her energy. They were standing at the center of a swirling maelstrom of golden energy that she had already gathered into her circle. John could see it now, and feel it crackling in the air around them. It was a heady feeling. So much magical energy gathered in one place.

He hoped it would be enough to deter the swarm of sea monsters that were violently churning the waters of the cove.

"John?" Ursula's voice came to him, filled with power but also somewhat hesitant.

"I'm here, honey," he was quick to assure her.

"When the dawn breaks in a few seconds, I'm going to turn around to face the cove. You'll have to get behind me."

"Which way do we turn? Clockwise?" he asked, watching the buildup of power with a good bit of awe. He had no idea she could call up such intense energy.

"Sounds good. Hold your hands out to the side, and I'll push lightly when it's time to go. We have to get the timing right, and I have to face the creature."

She sounded nervous. He knew it was up to him to help her through this test.

"You're not alone, Ursula. I'm right behind you, and if you agree, I can add a bit more power to what you've collected here. I'm connected to the forest and the earth—and as Alpha, to my people. I can give you access to at least some of that energy."

"Every little bit will help. Thank you, John." She sounded relieved, and he felt a moment of satisfaction, but they weren't out of the woods yet. "Almost time. Give me your hands."

Back to back, they clasped hands as Urse ticked off the seconds until she would unleash her spell. At the same time, John called on the magic that rested in his soul. It wasn't

60

something he did often, but most bear shifters could do rudimentary magic. It wasn't formal, by any means, but John knew how to tap into the power when he needed it. He did so now and fed it into the circle—and into the connection between himself and Ursula.

"John…" She sounded breathless, but in a good way. "Is that you doing that?"

"Roger that. I'm giving you what I can. We need every weapon in our arsenal against this monster. Is it okay?"

He needed to know if she could handle what he was dishing out. It was a hell of a time to experiment, but they'd been thrown into this, and he hadn't really realized what her spellwork would look like until he was in the middle of it.

"It's…" She seemed a little stunned for a moment, but he didn't think it was a bad thing. "It's fine. More than fine, actually. Your power feels…"

But her words halted as the sun's very first ray bled over the top of the mountains. He squeezed her hands.

"Show time," he whispered, even as he felt the pressure on his hand that told her it was time to reverse their positions.

They moved in a clockwise dance so that they traded positions. She let go of his hands as soon as she was facing the cove, and he turned around, standing right behind her. She was short enough that he could see right over the top of her head, which was just about perfect. If something bad happened, he could grab her and pull her back, out of the way.

She raised her hands and began to chant, the power inside the circle swirling and combining into a single entity that was larger than either of them. A bolt of pure Light and magic that she could launch out of the circle and into the cove.

Shouting a prayer to the Goddess over the roar of the power she'd gathered and the raucous splashing of the leviathan and its friends, she did just that. A magical wind swirled around them, lifting the long locks of her dark hair. She was the center of the storm that would rain down on the cove.

The bolt rose up into the sky, touching the first rays of dawn and then hammering down to strike at the water's edge and ripple outward.

It was like the sun itself was shining with the intensity of a laser, hitting from the point where she'd aimed, just on the edge of the shore, outward in a circular, rippling pattern.

The little monsters in the water tumbled back away from it, the smaller creatures in full retreat. The larger leviathan—the big daddy of them all—tried to fight it, but after a few moments, it too was pushed away, straining every bit of the way. It didn't go too far, but it was clear after a few minutes, while the sun rose and Ursula channeled its Light into the spell she had woven, that the leviathan had been successfully banished from at least a third of the cove.

For now.

John had no idea if it would last, but at least for now, this stretch of beach looked like the no-go zone he'd hoped would be created for that hideous animal. The leviathan clearly wasn't happy. It continued to rage in the waters beyond Ursula's influence for a few more minutes, but when the sun rose fully, it sank beneath the waves, as if in momentary defeat.

Or perhaps, strategic retreat.

John didn't like the implications of that. He knew the creature would come back even harder at them next time they tried to intervene like this. It knew what they were capable of now, and it would come prepared next time.

John stood behind Ursula as her chant wound down, ending with a prayer of thanks to the Mother of All for Her bounty and aid. He heard her words begin to slur a bit and realized that casting this spell had taken a toll on the *strega*. Ursula was trembling so much he could actually see her shoulders shaking.

And as the last words of her prayer left her mouth, she sagged.

She would have hit the ground, but John caught her, his

hands wrapping around her waist and pulling her back against his chest. She was depleted but still conscious, her eyelids heavy, but she still watched the sun's light hit the waters of the cove.

"It's done," she whispered. "That's all I can do for today."

"You did great, honey," he said quietly, next to her ear. "You've created a safe swath of beach and pushed the leviathan and its mini-me's out away from the shore. It's more than I thought would happen, and I'm very grateful."

He placed a small kiss on her temple, unable to resist the gesture of care. She was literally limp in his arms. She had given her all for the spell—and for the town and people he loved. She'd put herself out in a way he hadn't quite expected, and for that, she had earned a large portion of his respect and thanks.

"How long do you think this will last?" he asked, the thought occurring to him as he tucked her more tightly against his chest and they both watched the peaceful waters lapping at the protected section of rocky beach.

"As long as the sun rises in the east," she said, surprising him. "This sort of work is meant to stand the test of time. It is a sacred spell, known only to a few of us. It is my one true talent that sets me apart from other *strega*. Only a few of us can do permanent wards—or so Nonna insists." She chuckled weakly. "I really need to sleep now, John. Will you help me get back to bed?"

He was a little in awe of her now that he'd seen her power and realized just how strong and pure of heart she was to do this amazing thing for his town and people. If he wasn't much mistaken, he had just fallen a little bit in love with her.

"I'll take you anywhere you want to go, sweetheart, but tell me, is there any special ritual to getting out of this circle? Or can I just carry you over the salt line and be done with it?"

"Oh." She shook her head a little, and it lolled against his shoulder in the most endearing way. She looked a cross between drunk and exhausted, which made her seem a little loopy. He had to smile at the combination. "It needs to be broken from the inside," she said after a moment. "If you take me over to the edge, we can break it and collapse the barrier. Then everybody can come and go as they please. Somebody may want to scoop up whatever bits of the salt we can save for next time."

"I'll get my guys on it," he said, lifting her into his arms.

A little zing of satisfaction zapped through him as he scooped her up. She was light as a feather to him, and warm and womanly. Perfect. He liked the way she felt against him, and he liked it even better when her arm went around his shoulders and her face snuggled into the crook of his neck, like she'd been made just for him.

Dangerous thoughts, but after what he'd just seen, he was beyond caring for the moment.

He walked slowly, enjoying the feel of her in his arms, toward the edge of the circle closest to town. His men were stationed all around, some even creeping closer to the beach to check things over.

Zak, the deputy sheriff and highly trained sniper, was mirroring John's moves, a strange look on his face as he met them on the other side of the circle. It was only then that John realized that the barrier was very real. He couldn't really hear his men talking outside the line of salt. They all sounded muffled and indistinct. Like they were behind a wall.

That was some powerful magic, as far as John was concerned.

John stopped at the edge of the circle, looking down at Ursula. Her eyes were closed, but he knew she wasn't quite asleep yet.

"We're here, honey," he said softly. "What do I do to break the circle?"

"Oh." Her eyes blinked open. "Let me down, and I'll do it. This one is pretty strong, so I'm not sure it would respond well to you trying this. Only the caster should uncast something this big, I think."

John lowered her legs so that her feet touched the ground, but her knees were wobbly. He kept his arm around her shoulders, and his other hand steadied her at her waist.

"I need to reach down there," she said, pointing to the ground where the rock salt formed the base of the barrier.

John didn't want to let her go, so he lowered them both to the ground. Her knees folded neatly beneath her as he crouched, keeping his arm around her back for support.

"Is this okay?" he asked, his mouth near her ear.

They were so close together, his inner bear was getting a little drunk on the delicious scent of her skin. Like flower nectar and the first breath of spring, her scent enticed his wild side.

She reached down and spoke a prayer of thanks to the Goddess for lending Her strength to this circle of protection, then swept away a few inches of the salt, breaking the line. John actually felt the barrier collapse around them, the energy of it seeming to dissipate happily into the earth below as if going home.

And just like that, the sounds of the world came back to him. He could hear his men speaking in low voices to one another, and hear the wind in the trees and the splash of water on the rocky shore. It was as if the world had been unwrapped—or maybe his senses had—and everything was fresh and new, crisp and colorful.

John rose, lifting Ursula with him until they were both standing, facing Zak Flambeau.

"Tell me what you saw," John demanded, knowing that of all his men, Zak was the one who most often saw magic. He'd been raised in the bayous of Louisiana and knew more about human magic and voodoo than any of them.

"Helluva light show," Zak drawled. "Lit up the beach and water for a good long way. That wasn't a simple ward. That was something special, John. Something profound."

"Yeah," John agreed. "Apparently, Ms. Ricoletti is something a little different. She can cast permanent wards."

Zak whistled between his teeth, looking at Ursula with new respect. He even tipped his imaginary hat to the lady.

"We're blessed to have you here, ma'am," Zak said to her

with all seriousness. John was impressed.

Ursula seemed to blush, if John wasn't mistaken. "I'm glad I could help," was all she said.

"I'm going to take her back to her place. Post a watch and keep me informed of any developments," John ordered the small group of men who'd gathered closest.

He knew they'd keep him posted if there were any changes. Every last one of them were men he'd fought and bled alongside. They were brothers. Comrades in arms—and in their fur.

That they let him lead never failed to humble him. Bears weren't easily led. Highly magical and highly volatile, most bear shifters liked to roam alone, but this group—this special group of men tested in the crucible of battle many times over—was something very special. As was the woman in his arms, he was coming to understand.

John had picked her up when she'd stumbled and wasn't about to put her down again until there was a soft place to lay her. She was beat. He could see the fatigue written in her half-closed eyes and limp muscles. She was drained both physically and magically, and John grew concerned about the fact that they were supposed to do this all again just a bit over twenty-four hours from now.

The next ceremony was supposed to take place at high noon the following day. Judging by the way she looked and how much this dawn ceremony had taken out of her, John worried that she wouldn't be ready.

He wouldn't push her either. If she had to rest, she would rest. This could wait. No matter what her granny had said. He wasn't about to watch Ursula work herself to the bone—and possibly put her own life in more danger than she should. The whole project was inherently dangerous. Going into battle when you were already depleted was foolhardy at best. He wouldn't let her do it. She was too precious.

CHAPTER SIX

Amelia was at the door of the shop when John arrived with Ursula in his arms. She opened the door and held it for them while he carried her older sister inside. She was hopping from one foot to the other, looking worriedly at Ursula.

"Would you mind carrying her upstairs?" she asked John, cringing with anxiety.

Did she think he was going to say no? He'd have to teach her that he was one of the good guys. He wouldn't leave a lady, who was unconscious at this point, in the lurch.

"Lead the way," he told her, trying to sound as gentle as possible even though he knew a bit of a growl came through in his tone. He couldn't help it. All his protective instincts were in play now, and the idea that Amelia thought he wouldn't see her sister safely upstairs irked him.

She'd learn, though. John decided at that moment that he was going to stick around until both of the Ricoletti sisters learned what he was made of. Ursula, most of all.

Her opinion mattered to him...and to his bear. Now that was something different.

Never before had the bear really registered an opinion about a female—shifter or human. Suddenly, his furry half was sitting up and taking notice of every little move this magic woman made. *Strange.*

John, with his delicate burden, followed Amelia up the stairs and down the hall. He took only a cursory look around the apartment. He'd seen it unfurnished, of course. He'd been part of the building crew for this structure and had approved the blueprints, of course. He knew the layout, but he hadn't seen what the girls had done to the place since they moved in just a few short days ago.

He got the impression of color and light. Comfortable furniture and dainty knickknacks. A feminine, cozy space that invited rather than repulsed him.

But Amelia was leading him down the hall to the front bedroom. That must be the one Ursula had claimed. It was only slightly larger than the bedroom that sat next to it, but it was right on the street, overlooking the cove. It had the best view.

Sure enough, she opened the door and led him into the room. Amelia pulled back the covers on Ursula's bed before John set her down on the pale lilac sheets. The faint scent of flowers and fresh linen hit his nose, making him want to smile. It was an innocent smell that reminded him of fresh meadows and clothes drying on the line when he was a cub. It was a happy scent that brought back good memories.

John laid Ursula down and stepped back, allowing Amelia room to check on her sister. She looked worried as she put one hand over her sister's forehead and closed her own eyes, seeming to mutter a bit just under her breath, so low that not even John's shifter-sharp hearing could hear what she said.

A moment later, Amelia opened her eyes and smiled. She looked up at John, a relieved expression on her face.

"She's okay. She just needs to sleep it off for a while." Amelia got up and walked toward the door to the bedroom. "Can I offer you a cup of tea? Or something stronger?" she asked politely.

John didn't want to leave. In fact, he didn't want to leave Ursula's bedroom, but he couldn't very well just sit there and watch her sleep. Amelia's invitation gave him an excuse to stay in the apartment at least. He'd take what he could get.

Tea would take time to brew, so tea it was.

"That sounds great," he said quietly, so as not to disturb Ursula's sleep.

He followed Amelia out the door and down the hall, back toward the kitchen that was at the other end of the apartment. There were still boxes everywhere, but the important parts of the household had already been unpacked, and the kitchen looked like it was fully equipped.

He'd been in the kitchen before, of course, when they'd had dinner, but he hadn't seen much of the rest of the apartment before. The sisters had done a nice job with their decorating, and John said as much to Amelia, earning a smile from her as she bustled around, making the tea.

When they were both seated around the small kitchen table, holding mugs of steaming tea, she finally seemed to relax a bit.

"It went well, Amelia," he told her. "You should've seen her go. The power she called up was really impressive." He hoped that by stating his impressions about what her sister had done, he would get Amelia to open up a bit more to him.

"Yeah, I could feel the whammy when she released it from the circle. I couldn't go out because sister dear warded the doors and windows specifically against my leaving before she returned. She locked me in," she said, sounding horribly offended.

John tried unsuccessfully to smother his smile.

"Don't you laugh," she scolded with some humor. "I wanted to be there for her, but she made it so I couldn't even get out of the building. The stinker."

"She loves you." John shrugged, thinking it was obvious. "She wanted to protect you."

"I get it, but it still stinks," Amelia groused. "First Nonna tells me not to help, and then, Urse goes one further as if I'm not to be trusted."

"Well, if she hadn't sealed you in, would you have been out there, where you probably shouldn't have been?" John challenged with a grin.

"Yeah, okay. I probably would have." She looked chagrinned as she sipped at her tea.

"Believe me, she couldn't afford the distraction of worrying about you," he told her, not unkindly. "That spell was like nothing I've ever seen before."

"You saw it?" She sounded intrigued.

"I was in the circle with her," he admitted.

"Really?" Amelia shot him an impressed expression. "I'm surprised, but glad you were there for her. She always tries to protect everyone else and takes too much on herself."

John had to chuckle. "I've been accused of that very same thing once or twice myself."

"The two of you are a pair," she said absently, but the words made him stop and think.

Were they? Meant to be a pair? Hmm.

Possibly.

They sipped their tea in silence for a few minutes before Amelia put her empty mug down on the table and sat up straight. She looked at him, as if wondering how far she could trespass on his good nature.

"Do you think you can stay here for a few more minutes and keep an eye on Urse? I don't want her to wake up and have nobody here. She'll worry about me, and she doesn't need to do that right now," she said in a nervous rush. "I want to go over to the bakery and get some of her favorite breads and pastries for when she wakes up. Believe it or not, this kind of magical work can burn a lot of calories, and it's important to keep her fueled up if she's going to do this again tomorrow."

"I'll stay. Take your time. I'll look out for her."

"Great. The wards came down when she crossed the threshold, so I can finally get out of here for a few minutes." Amelia was gathering her bag and cleaning up the tea stuff, bustling around before she headed out. "Everything is where you would expect it in here. If you're hungry, help yourself to anything in the fridge or cupboards. I'll be back in about twenty minutes."

"It's okay," John told her. "I'm in no hurry. In fact, I'd like to talk to your sister when she wakes up, just to satisfy myself that she's okay, so don't rush."

"She may not wake up for a while," Amelia said, a worried expression on her face.

"That's okay." John shrugged. "If she does, I'd like to talk to her if she's up to it. If not, I'll come back later when she is awake, if that's okay."

"Oh, sure," Amelia immediately agreed. "She'll probably want to talk to you about the plan for tomorrow's ceremony anyway, so that'll work." Amelia headed for the door to the stairs and headed out. "See you in a bit. And thanks."

John just nodded, watching her go.

He cleaned up his half-finished mug of tea, draining the rest of it down the sink before he felt the pull toward the front bedroom again that had never quite left since he'd placed Ursula on her bed. Why he was suddenly picturing her there, wearing quite a bit less than the jeans and sweater she'd been wearing that morning, he really didn't want to examine.

He only knew he had to go check on her.

Following the pull, he walked silently up the hall, to the door at the end that beckoned.

Urse was just opening her eyes as the door to her bedroom opened and John was there. Was she dreaming? She blinked a few times as he walked closer.

"John?" she asked, her voice a bit weaker than she liked.

He came closer. "I'm right here, honey. How are you feeling?"

"Like I got run over. But it's to be expected." She sat up in bed, realizing only then that she was in her own bedroom. The last thing she remembered, he'd been carrying her and they were outside. "Fill me in on what I missed."

"Nothing much," he said, surprising her by sitting on the side of her bed, facing her. It was close...intimate. More than she'd expected. "I carried you in. Your sister complained about you warding the doors and windows, but apparently the wards dropped when you came through. She went down to the bakery to get some treats she said you deserved, and I agreed to keep an eye on you so you wouldn't wake up alone. No news from my guys, which means everything is just as we left it." He took one of her hands, gripping it lightly. "That was a hell of a thing you did out there. I had no idea you were that powerful."

She felt a bit of discomfort. "I don't suppose that's a good thing. You probably want us gone even more now, right?"

"On the contrary," he surprised her by saying. He scooched a little closer to her, adding his other hand to the one that was already wrapped warmly around hers. "I like knowing you can hold your own, and after being inside that circle with you, I'm in no doubt as to your basic nature. Your magic feels pure and good. You can be a strong ally of my people, if that's your inclination, but either way, you're welcome here. I'll square it with the rest of the guys, but I think after they saw what you did out there to protect us, they won't need much convincing."

Urse breathed a sigh of relief. She didn't know exactly when it had happened, but Grizzly Cove had begun to feel like home, and she wanted to stay.

"I'm glad," she said, feeling emotional about his turnaround. "And I promise…we're the good guys. We don't have any hidden agendas or sinister plans. We don't even do a lot of magic most of the time. Just when it's needed. As you see, it takes a bit out of you, so we've been taught to only act when it's really necessary."

"You don't have to explain. After what I witnessed in that circle, I trust you. And that's not something I say easily." He tilted his head, his voice dropping low. "You've earned both my trust and my respect."

"I've always respected you, John," she whispered, feeling the air around them warm with a strange sort of intimacy.

Silence fell, and he drew closer. Was he going to…?

Oh, yeah.

John's lips touched hers, and all coherent thought fled,

replaced by pure feeling.

He kissed like a dream. Like a conquering hero who knew how to seduce. Like the masterful Alpha he was. And she was drawn in, the willing partner to his passion.

Something ignited between them. Her blood heated instantly, her heart going from zero to sixty in no seconds flat. It was fast and furious, passionate and powerful. It was unlike any response she'd had to a man before. John was unique. His kiss made her want oh-so-much-more.

His tongue seduced, his taste zinged through her body like a drug, and she was an instant addict. He moved his hands over her body, at first just holding her, then growing bolder, touching her through her clothes.

When his big hand cupped her breast, she wanted nothing more than for the layers of fabric separating his warm palm from her skin to be gone. If she could have twitched her nose and made her clothes disappear, she would have, but that wasn't one of her powers. No, if she wanted skin on skin, they were going to have to do it the old fashioned way.

Impatiently, she pushed at his shoulders, trailing her hands downward to the hem of his stretchy golf shirt. She liked the way he dressed—clean and simple. And easy to take off.

He seemed to get the message and moved back for the short moment it took to remove his shirt, pulling it up over his head. The sexy six pack abdominals revealed by his too-quick striptease made her mouth water. She wanted so badly to touch.

When he recaptured her lips with his, she allowed her hands to roam. He was hard and muscled all over, inviting her fingers to linger.

She liked the sexy growl that vibrated through his chest against her palms. It awoke something within her—an animal spirit she could trace directly back to that long-ago bear shifter in her lineage. She didn't notice it often, but every once in a while, she felt the presence of it, way down in her soul.

Only now, it was much closer. It was as if being around

John had woken the grizzly. It wanted to be near its own kind. Well, one in particular.

Her hidden inner bear was riled…in a good way, and she wanted to hear John growl in that special way again. More than that, though, she wanted to feel his hands on her skin.

Like a mind reader, John finally got around to pushing the light jacket she'd worn off her shoulders. She let it slide down her arms and pushed it off her hands to fall behind her. His fingers toyed with the hem of her T-shirt, and she covered one of his large hands to urge him onward.

They broke apart again so he could pull the shirt up and off her body, leaving her only in her bra. She wanted that gone too, but he seemed to want to take it slow. He kissed her again, making her his willing slave. She'd do anything he wanted. He'd mastered her mouth, and she couldn't wait to see how the rest of her body would react to his advances.

Then he reached around her to unhook the clasp of her bra. *Yes!*

The thin straps were tugged slowly down her shoulders, and then, the cups were peeled away, one at a time. All the while, he kept kissing her, learning the shape of her body with his hands and skilled fingers.

She loved every minute of it. Every touch. Every caress.

And then, John moved away, letting her go. Urse tried to follow, but he pushed gently against her shoulder.

"Your sister is home," he told her softly. "She's coming up the stairs."

Now that was a mood killer, right there. Urse felt like a panicked teenager caught necking at the drive-in. John seemed to understand. He rose and put his shirt back on, then ran a quick hand through his hair.

"I'll go out and meet her, give her a sitrep and tell her you're awake. Five minutes enough?" he asked, already heading toward the door of her bedroom.

Thank goodness at least one of them was thinking. She nodded, already scrambling to find her clothes. Mel was sharp-eyed, and the last thing Urse wanted was to sit through her teasing, if she realized what she and the hunky mayor had just been up to. It wasn't likely she'd be able to fool Mellie for long, but she'd give it her best shot.

This thing with John was too new. Too fragile. Too uncertain.

Would he want a repeat? Had they crossed over into a new sort of relationship just now? Or was this a one-off? A moment out of time, never to be repeated.

She just didn't know. She wasn't sure where she stood with him, but she did know, for certain, that she wanted more.

John had just shown her things about herself that she hadn't known. He'd somehow bared her soul and left her feeling stronger and more empowered as a woman than she'd ever felt before. He was a good man, who knew how to make a woman feel good…in more than just the obvious, sexual, way. He made her feel good about herself.

And that was something she hadn't expected.

Nor had she expected that he was attracted to her. The last she knew he was mad at her for lying—by omission—about her magical nature. Okay, maybe not *mad*. He'd seemed more disappointed and sort of annoyed because he didn't seem to know what to do about the situation. Not that he'd have to *do* anything. She was a witch. So what?

That wasn't to say that she didn't understand where he was coming from. He'd built this town for shifters, and everything he'd said indicated that he hadn't really thought about other magical races wanting to join him and his group of bears in the new settlement. Really, though, he probably should've thought about it a little more. If there was one thing she knew for a fact, magic often attracted magic.

And bears were some of the most magical of shifters, according to everything she'd been taught. Many of them were shamans and mages in their own right. Holy men and women. Priests and priestesses in various cultures. Not all, of course, but many, according to Nonna and her other teachers who'd sometimes mentioned shifters.

Urse got out of bed and went to her dresser—and more importantly the big mirror above it. She looked flushed, but maybe that could be explained by having just woken up or something? She did her best to make sure all her clothes were in the right places and her hair tidy before she turned toward the door to her bedroom, which John had thoughtfully closed.

Even Urse could hear Mellie coming down the hall now. Thank goodness for John's sharp shifter hearing. If he hadn't given her a few minutes to get herself together...or if Mellie had caught them in the act... Well, it wouldn't have been the end of the world, but Urse would have been really embarrassed.

As it was, she just wanted to hug the knowledge of what they'd done—not that it was all that much, darn it—to herself for a while. It was too new to share just yet, or put on public display, even accidentally.

"Urse?" Mellie tapped on the door before opening it a tiny bit. When she saw Urse standing by the dresser, she opened it all the way and walked in. Mellie came straight to her and hugged her tight. "You had me worried, sis," she said somewhat raggedly.

"I'm okay," Urse reassured her little sister. "It just drained me a bit, but I'm feeling better now. You know how it goes."

"Boy, do I." Mellie let her go and then hiked herself up to sit on the edge of the dresser, looking Urse over. "And you have to do this a few more times, right? Do you think you can handle it?" Mellie looked concerned.

"I'll have to, but honestly, it wasn't too bad. John was with me. He was right there in the circle with me." She still couldn't really get over that. She'd thought she'd be all alone, but he'd been her partner, her protector and her anchor. "He even added quite a bit of power to the spell, which I definitely didn't expect going in. He made it a lot stronger and a lot more effective. Plus, I wasn't as scared with him in there with me. I figured if I screwed up and those tentacles came for me, John would help me fight them off."

"I wanted to be the one to help you," Mellie insisted in a quiet, hurt tone.

"You know you can't. Not only did Nonna forbid it, but you know as well as I do that my kind of magic isn't your strong point. Nor can I help you with the potions you're going to need to work on for the second phase of this operation."

"Second phase?" John's query came from the doorway. The man moved so silently he'd snuck up on them.

Urse looked at him, his endearingly raised eyebrow invited her to answer, but her heart was racing—both from being surprised by his presence and a little excited about seeing him again after what they'd done just a few minutes ago. Was she blushing? She really hoped she wasn't blushing.

"Come on," she said, going for distraction and heading for the hall. She'd have to pass John to get into the hallway, but at least Mellie wouldn't see the telltale flush Urse just *knew* was racing to her cheeks. "I'm hungry. Let's nibble on something, and we'll go over what comes next."

She led the way toward the kitchen, glad when she heard them following. She had to regain control of herself, and the situation.

Urse busied herself making a sandwich at the kitchen counter while the other two took seats at the table. She looked at John, shrugged, and decided to make two sandwiches—one for her and an extra-giant-sized one for him. They'd both been up since before dawn, and it had to be mid-morning now, if not close to lunchtime.

Without a word, she placed the plate she'd made up for him in front of John, then took her own seat next to him at the table. Mellie was on one end of the rectangular table, unpacking a bag from the bakery and putting her purchases on a platter.

Urse took a bite out of her sandwich, chewed and swallowed before she spoke again. Yum. She'd needed that. The magical work had taken a lot out of her, both emotionally and physically. She needed to replace the many calories she'd used.

"Okay." She wiped her mouth with her napkin. "So, Phase Two. That would be Mellie's part. Tell him, Mel." She introduced the topic and let her sister take it away while Urse concentrated on stuffing her sandwich in her mouth.

CHAPTER SEVEN

John was intrigued as Amelia explained more about her work with potions and the research she would have to do before implementing her part of the plan. Apparently, there were herbs and precious commodities to be gathered and blessed, then prepared in just the right way. Potion work, she told him, shouldn't be undertaken quickly. A hasty potion could very well have disastrous consequences.

He'd had no idea. Then again, John hadn't ever spent any time with magic users. Not good ones, anyway. There had been the occasional bad guy who flung magic at them when he'd been leading his Spec Ops team, but John hadn't stopped to chat before tearing the bad guys apart.

He was learning all sorts of things about good magic today. These two young *strega* had really opened his eyes. And Ursula, in particular, had made him think about things beyond magic and managing the town. She'd made him think about personal things. Things about his own future.

John hadn't given his personal life much thought lately. He sort of figured the town had to come first. When that was up and running, he had hoped that a suitable female grizzly shifter might miraculously show up and be his mate. It was more than a little ridiculous, when he stopped to think about it.

Ursula was real. She was here. And his bear was making noises inside his mind that led him to believe she might be the one.

That was even more ridiculous, but there it was. The Alpha bear couldn't mate with a mage and keep his position. He doubted his men would stand for it. They all distrusted magic other than their own. Shifter magic was one thing. Ursula's kind of magic... That was something else entirely, and most likely wouldn't be acceptable to the vast majority of his people. The Alpha pair would, presumably, lead the others—even if bears weren't easily lead—and they both had to be bears, right? Not a mage and bear pair, even if Ursula did have bear blood way back in her ancestry. It was too faint to count. She couldn't shift. She was a mage. A *strega*.

It was the principle of the thing, more than anything else. Humans were acceptable as mates. The Baker sisters were living proof of the concept. Magic users? Not so much.

But John had always believed that rules were made to be broken. So maybe the rest of the guys wouldn't follow his lead anymore. So what? Big deal. They weren't always the best at following orders anyway. It would be worth stepping down as leader of this ragtag Clan to find that most elusive of desires. A true mate was worth any sacrifice.

If Ursula Ricoletti turned out to be his true mate, all bets were off. John would move hell and high water to keep her, regardless of whether she was a witch or not. Nothing mattered but that deep, true bond that he had seen between his parents, and even between the three Baker sisters and the sons of bitches lucky enough to claim them as their mates.

John was happy for those guys, but seeing their happiness had made him yearn for the same. He honestly hadn't thought it would happen for him. At least not right away. Maybe in a few years, after the town was settled. But it looked like the Mother of All had different ideas.

Maybe.

This was all speculation on his part. He'd have to get a lot closer to Ursula to know for sure.

If she was really his mate, then so be it.

"Thanks for the sandwich," John said, finishing the delicious concoction Ursula had placed before him without asking. "It was really great."

"No problem. I figured you'd be hungry by now," Ursula replied, sounding nonchalant. But John knew better. She'd been watching him covertly the whole time they'd been eating.

"I'd like to discuss plans for tomorrow's exercise, if you're still up for it," John said to her, searching her eyes for signs of weariness. She still looked really tired. "But we can do that tonight, if you'd rather rest now."

Ursula smothered a yawn. "Yeah, I'm sorry, but I think I'm going to have to go back to sleep for a bit. I'll be fine for tomorrow. I just have to recharge. Can you come back later? How about joining us for dinner? We can talk then."

John agreed and took his leave without having another chance to talk to Ursula alone. He left, knowing he had a lot of work to do before he could keep that dinner appointment.

Might as well get to it.

The very first item on his list was to check in with his men and get their impressions of the efficacy of Ursula's spell. By now his men should have measured the effective zone and have any number of observations to report. He made his way down the street to the new town hall they had built and went directly to the war room they'd put in place for just this kind of thing.

Ostensibly, it was just a large conference room, but every one of his ex-soldiers knew this was the place they'd chosen and set up to be the primary nerve center if there was a problem in town. There was a secondary and even a tertiary site available too—the secondary being in John's home. That had been their primary meeting place until they'd finished the town hall. The third choice was now the a/v room in Brody's house.

All three locations had state-of-the-art computer systems and satellite link-ups. John and Brody had each paid for and set up their own equipment. Most of the ex-Spec Ops guys who had settled here had as much tech in their dens as they could buy or scrounge. The stuff at the town hall had been a group initiative, paid for out of Clan funds generated by the various businesses in the town.

When John arrived at the war room, there was a sitrep waiting for him, and the news was good. Ursula's magic that morning had protected about a third of the cove's beach. The men had run tests to see how far the protections extended and had mapped out where the wards left off on a map of the cove.

John was impressed all over again with what Ursula had done. And she would do it all again tomorrow, which was even more amazing. The town would owe her a huge debt of gratitude, and he hoped that meant the guys would be willing to accept her, and her sister, among them.

Surely, she'd earned their respect already, just from the morning's effort. In time, maybe they'd be willing to let the two *strega* stay in Grizzly Cove, as a sort of reward for having been so willing to help protect the place. John could see that happening, and he'd do all in his power to get the others to agree. After what he'd learned this morning about her abilities, Ursula would be a good ally for the Clan.

And personally, he might just have glimpsed his future. If the lovely—and powerful—Ursula turned out to be his mate…well…either she would stay here or John would give up on the Grizzly Cove project entirely. He'd sell his land, which might take some time, since he was the biggest landowner in the area. But he'd sell out and leave. Let the others keep the cove running, if they could. If he had a chance at a mate and the others didn't accept her, he'd leave and never look back.

Mates were precious. More important than social experiments, towns, friends or anything else. They were hope. They were a reward for faith, and a promise of love.

But all that was for the future. Right now, they had a sea monster problem on their hands, and John needed all the data he could gather before tonight so he could help Ursula plan the most effective attack for tomorrow. His resolve firmly set, he went to work collating all the reports from his men and searching for anything that might help them tomorrow.

Back above the bookstore, Urse called Nonna to talk about the events of the morning and get any advice the older *strega* might have for the following day. It felt good to hear Nonna's voice and even better to receive praise for what she'd done that morning. Even in San Francisco, Nonna had been able to feel the power of the ward going up several hundred miles north on the coast.

Nonna had been looking for it, of course. She thought perhaps other magic users might have noticed the momentary surge of magical energy in the Pacific Northwest, but such things happened from time to time and probably wouldn't draw too much attention. Then again, Nonna had warned her that the power surges that would take place over the next days while Urse worked might attract attention.

With any luck, it would be benign entities noticing the surges, but if something evil happened to see it and want to know what it was that could generate such power, Urse and Mellie would have to be on guard—and Urse should warn the bears too, Nonna advised. She also reminded Urse of a few of the safeguards she had taught her granddaughter that could add a little protective kick to the spells Urse would weave next.

Taking mental notes, Urse was glad for her grandmother's advice and encouragement. Most of all, Nonna reminded her not to worry too much. Things would happen as they were meant to unfold. And then, Nonna had done something Urse hadn't expected. She'd asked about *her* bear.

Stymied by the very deliberate wording, Urse had protested. "He's not *my* bear."

"Come now, *bella*. Didn't he add his power to yours?" Nonna insisted.

"Well...yes. He was inside the circle with me, and he offered to add the power of his Clan to the spell. That's why it was a bit stronger than I expected."

"Child, that sort of thing doesn't happen easily. Tell me, did your energies mesh easily? No effort required to make them work together?" Nonna sounded a little too smug, but Urse didn't really know where she was going with these questions.

"Well, yeah. I mean, once he started channeling energy into the circle, it seemed to get along well with mine. It twined and sort of merged, each part strengthening the other," she said, remembering the way the magic had flowed so easily together. It was actually something really beautiful to witness, and if she hadn't been so scared about fighting the leviathan, she would have enjoyed it a lot more.

Nonna made a *tsking* sound at her through the phone line. "That doesn't happen often, or easily. If your bear's magic can merge with yours, that means something significant for you both as individuals. You are compatible. *Very* compatible. Some might say, you are destined to work together in magic, and perhaps in life."

"No way." Urse was nonplussed. Was Nonna saying John might be her match? Her... What did the shifters call it again? Her *mate*?

"I cannot say for certain," Nonna said quietly, amusement clear in her tone. "Such things are for the Lady to decide, but do not be surprised if your bear starts making advances."

For just a moment, Urse felt like a teenager caught necking with her high school crush. John had made *advances*, as Nonna put it. Had they been serious? He'd kissed her.

The question was...had he been thinking about starting something serious? Or had it just been an impulse of the moment?

Urse finished the call with her grandmother shortly after that, returning to bed with the memory of John's kiss whirling through her mind until she fell asleep. She dreamed of a big, soft, ferocious bear who let her rest her head against his furry chest, protecting her as she slept.

John returned right around dinnertime to find Ursula much improved. In fact, she was preparing the food right alongside her sister. If he hadn't known better, he would never have guessed she'd been through so much that very morning.

Amelia had let him in and walked with him up the stairs, chattering all the way. She was still on edge around him, but he guessed that was to be expected. The younger sister hadn't spent much time around him since the big revelation. She probably thought he was still angry about it.

He'd had a bit of time to think about the entire situation this afternoon, and he'd come to some startling realizations. First among them was that he no longer wished for the *strega* sisters to leave Grizzly Cove. He'd fight every last bear in the town if he had to, but he wanted them to stay. Especially Ursula.

She felt important to him. He wasn't one hundred percent sure what she meant to him yet, but he wanted the time to find out. Keeping them both here was the only way he would get it.

So that was one thing. Another thought had occurred to him as well. With so much shifter magic concentrated in one town, they'd be foolish not to ally themselves with Others who had proven trustworthy.

John had already formed an alliance with the Master vampire of Seattle. Master Hiram was the silent partner funding the construction of Zak's restaurant, after all. Hiram had literally washed up on their beach, wounded gravely, his immortal existence in peril. He had proven himself to John and his men as a being of restraint and reason.

John was glad of the connection. Their new relationship had already proved mutually beneficial. Hiram was an ancient being of great power, sworn to the side of Light.

Now the Ricoletti sisters had appeared in his town, out of the blue. Ursula had put herself on the line this morning, to protect the cove and its inhabitants. She, too, was proving to be a being who could command immense magical power.

John hadn't realized it before. Ursula was a very attractive woman, but she didn't look on the outside like a true force to be reckoned with. He'd only seen that side of her when it was pressed into service this morning, to protect others.

Her work today had been one of self-sacrifice, in the goal of defeating evil and protecting the innocent. That was something John could truly respect. It was, after all, a creed by which he had lived most of his life.

John had gone into the military for just that reason. He'd been an idealist, wanting to right wrongs and take down bad guys. He'd done his fair share of that all over the world, alongside most of the residents of this new town. This place was his very own social experiment, and it was time he broadened the horizons of his dream to include Others he hadn't expected, but needed to welcome, in order to make this place and secure as possible.

Ursula and Amelia could contribute. In fact, they were all set to contribute their power and skills, not knowing whether or not they would be welcome to stay. They were willing to expend their magical energy to protect those who might just as easily turn around and throw them out of town after they were done.

That didn't sit right with John. No way was he going to let anyone run these girls out of town on a rail. They were doing their part. Hell, they were doing more than their fair share.

Ursula was laying permanent wards against evil all around the cove. That still boggled John's mind. He hadn't known such things could even be done in this day and age, when there was so little true magic left in the world of man.

She was making the place safe, not just for her own sake—for her time here—but for all time. That was an incredibly valuable and selfless gift.

He would see that she was allowed to stay here and enjoy the benefits of her work. Come hell or high water.

Then again, if the leviathan had its way, maybe both would

happen. And then, they'd all be sunk.

Urse didn't know what to think when John walked into the kitchen. He just stood there for a few minutes, watching her, as Mellie went down the hall to answer the phone.

Did he now regret what had passed between them earlier in the day? Or, like her, did he simply not know what to say?

He managed to answer both of her questions without uttering a sound. He just walked right up to her, took her in his arms, and kissed her, right there in the middle of the kitchen.

Now that was the kind of greeting she could get behind.

She was just getting into his kiss when he pulled back. He looked down at her, searching her gaze.

"You okay?" he asked. She got the feeling he meant more by the simple question than just an inquiry about her health.

She nodded. "Yeah," she answered breathlessly, looking deep into his golden brown eyes.

"Do you want to keep this between us for now?"

Was he asking her—in that growly, intimate tone that made her insides clench—if she wanted to go public with their change in status from acquaintances to...whatever this was between them now? She had no idea what to do. Mellie would tease her, but if John was serious and this went somewhere, it would be worth it. But...maybe not right away. Not until she knew a little more about where they were going.

"Maybe?" Did he look disappointed, or was she imagining that? "What do you want to do?" she asked quickly.

He growled. Actually growled. Why did she find that so damn sexy? And why did something wild down deep in her soul want to growl back in agreement?

"I don't care who knows, but I figured you might have some feelings on the matter."

"Where are we going with this?" She tilted her head, knowing her question had come out on a breathy note. She couldn't help it. John made her breathless, just by being near.

"Anywhere you want. All the way, I hope. I'm not playing

with you, I swear. I haven't been involved with a woman in a long time, but there's just something about you, Ursula. Something…almost magnetic. You pull both halves of me toward you. If I'm honest, you did since the first time we met."

"Why didn't you say anything before now? Or are you secretly turned on by my magic?" She turned a sly grin on him, teasing a bit, but also really curious about his somewhat sudden turnaround. This was happening fast, but she was very attracted to him, so now that he seemed interested, her inner hussy was all over it.

He sighed. "Your magic complicates things, but after what I saw today, I know it's a big part of you. Honestly, you impressed the hell out of me, honey. I had no idea you were so…amazing."

A little corner of her heart warmed at his praise.

"But it's not why I'm no longer fighting the pull. The more I'm around you, the less I'm able to stay away. I hadn't planned on this, but now that you're here…I can't help myself." He shrugged a little, then smiled that devastating grin that had attracted her to him from the beginning. "Nor do I want to stay away. It's stupid to fight fate, or magic, or whatever this is. All I know is you make me happy, and you make my bear stand up and take notice, which it hasn't done in a long, long time. And never like this. This feels…serious."

Had he gulped before that last word? Had she, after hearing it?

Serious. Wow.

Yeah, that's how it felt for her too. Good to know they were both on the same page—and it was amazing to hear such things from this man after such a short time. Could it be real? Or was the stress of the situation getting the better of her?

"I'm not normally an impulsive person…" she began, unsure how to express her feelings. It was all so complicated. "And I'm not sure if this is real, or something brought about by the strange circumstances we're facing."

He let her go, making her wish she could call her words back. Had she hurt his feelings? Damn. That's not what she'd intended.

John ran one hand through his golden brown hair as he leaned back against the kitchen counter.

"So you think this is stress-induced?" he finally asked, his eyes shadowed and unreadable.

"I don't know," she admitted. "Maybe?"

John let out a gusty sigh. "Honey, I know pressure and stress. I've lived with both for many years as the leader of my team. I know my reactions, and I know this one isn't the least bit determined by the stress of the situation. But the same apparently doesn't go for you, and I'm trying to be patient with that. You're not a shifter, and from what I understand, it isn't the same for humans. It's probably not the same for *strega* either." He sighed again, a little less energetically, and a small smile played around his lips. "Whatever happens, we'll figure it out. I'll just have to be patient. But don't ask me to leave your side. Not now. Not while you're in danger. For now, my place is with you when you're working to protect this cove. Whether or not I'm there outside of those times is completely up to you. That's all the room I can give you."

Urse nodded slowly, realizing how much of a concession the dominant Alpha grizzly shifter had just made. He was toning down his protective instincts for her—at least a little. That had to mean something special. He was trying to accommodate the fact that she wasn't a shifter.

"Okay. We can work with that," she said. "For right now, let's just play it cool in front of Mellie. Otherwise, she'll tease me all night, and I'll never get to sleep."

"Looks like you two are on your own," Mellie called as she breezed down the hallway, already shrugging into her jacket. "That was Tina on the phone. I called her earlier about some herbs I need, and she invited me to dinner over at the bakery so I can look at their roof garden and see if any of their plants are something I can use. They put in a little greenhouse section so they've even got some stuff that's out of season, which could be an enormous help. If it works out, I'll need to harvest at midnight, so I might just stay over there in their guest room. Tina said it was okay. Zak's going to meet me at the front door and walk me over." Mellie rolled her eyes as she headed for the door, her bag slung over her shoulder. "It's all overkill, if you ask me, but he made me promise to wait for *an escort*, as he put it." She shook her head, barely drawing a breath in her excited chatter. "Never thought I'd need a police escort to walk down Main Street."

"It's for your own protection," John put in. Apparently, he was a miracle worker because Urse had never really been able to get a word in edgewise when Mel was all hyped up like this.

"Yeah, I get it. But Urse made this stretch of the beach safe this morning. It'll be okay. You'll see." Mellie's unwavering confidence in Urse's abilities made her smile.

"Call and let me know if you're going to stay overnight," she managed to sneak in before Mel got going again.

"Okay. But I'll probably end up staying. Their garden is to die for, and the new greenhouse sounds just about perfect. We should consider doing something similar up top." Mellie finally slowed down, no doubt recalling the trouble they were in with John and the town. "If we stay, that is."

"You're staying," John said in a firm voice, surprising Urse and Mellie alike. "If I have anything to say about it, you're staying. And if the others decide you need to go, you won't be going alone."

"You mean…?" Urse looked at him, hardly daring to believe his words.

"I mean, if the rest of the guys can't appreciate what you're doing for this town, then they're not the bears I thought they were. If that happens, I'm leaving too, and I'll be certain to tell them exactly why before I go."

"But John—" Urse protested just as a knock sounded from downstairs, followed by the chime of the doorbell from the shop's front door. Zak, no doubt, had arrived.

"That's my police escort," Mellie said softly into the raging silence. She looked uncomfortable, but also still keyed up to see the Baker sisters' greenhouse.

"Go, Mel," Urse said softly. "We'll talk about all of this later. And say hi to Zak and Tina for me."

"Do me a favor and don't mention what I've just said. I want to see how the guys react without the pressure of an ultimatum, okay?" John asked Mellie.

Mel nodded slowly. "That makes sense. Nobody will hear it from me. I promise."

"Fair enough." John nodded with seeming satisfaction. "Safe travels and good hunting, Amelia."

Mellie said goodbye and rushed down the stairs.

CHAPTER EIGHT

"Alone at last." John turned to Urse, waggling his eyebrows as he grinned. "This is an unexpected treat."

"Is it?" Urse went to stir the pots on the stove, making sure everything was simmering and that nothing would burn while they talked about the bomb he'd just dropped. "Did you mean it? That you'd leave the town you created if the rest of the townsfolk forced us to leave?"

John stepped closer to her, his hands going to her waist. "I meant every word. I had a long time to think this afternoon, and that was one of the things I decided. If the guys can't see how good you are and how much you're giving of yourself to help protect them, then they're not people I want to be around anymore. This entire social experiment will just have to go on without me."

"But you're the heart of this town, John. Even I can see that. You're the star around which all the others revolve. You're their sun. Their leader. Their...Alpha. What you've built here is special. Almost sacred. I wouldn't want you to give all this up because of me and my sister."

John tucked her against his chest, holding her loosely, but letting her feel his reassuring warmth.

"It's early days yet. I have no idea how this is all going to work out—with the town, with the leviathan, with you and me…" He kissed the crown of her head, offering comfort, and perhaps taking a little for himself at the same time. "Let's just see where it goes. If the guys are half the men I think they are, then there won't be any question about forcing you to leave town, and the issue will never come up. I just wanted it to be clear that if you go, I go."

"Does that mean we go…like…*together*?" she dared to ask in a small voice.

"I don't know the answer to that one either, just yet, but it's sure starting to feel that way, isn't it?" He leaned back, seeking her gaze with his.

She was caught by his gaze. Captured. Willingly. Happily.

"Yeah," she said slowly, as time spun out. "It's beginning to feel that way."

John smiled, his expression holding more than a hint of relief. "I'm glad to hear you say that. This is all uncharted territory for me. I don't know how it is for humans or magic users, but shifters tend to know pretty quickly…and permanently."

"Permanently?" she squeaked on that last syllable, but who could blame her? They hadn't even gone on a real date yet and he was talking *permanent*. Like forever. *Whoa.*

Just at that moment, the timer dinged. Dinner was ready. Saved by the bell.

John backed off, and she hated the disappointment on his face, but she was powerless to do anything about it. Not yet. He'd blindsided her a bit with his talk of forever. Her brain had to catch up with her heart.

Was that bad?

She wasn't sure. Actually, she wasn't sure about anything right now. She needed time—and a little space—to think.

"I have to check the roast," she said softly. "The timer…"

John stepped away, giving her the room she needed to move toward the oven, from which delicious aromas were wafting. Urse checked, and luckily, everything was ready. She began pulling pans from the oven and getting things ready to serve. John moved silently at her side, helping, which surprised her at first, but he turned out to be very useful in the kitchen.

It didn't take long to get everything on the table. They sat down together and began eating, making only small talk about the food by some unspoken agreement. Things had gotten a little too heavy, too fast for Urse's groggy brain to keep up with. She had to chew on John's revelations and figure out what she thought besides a breathless, *really*?

Something purely emotional inside her was jumping up and down like a two year old on a sugar high. Her adult brain was flabbergasted and unable to keep up with the emo chattering.

About halfway through the meal, John brought up the spell she was going to perform tomorrow at noon. Glad for the change of topic, Urse told him about her plans as best she could.

"The noon ceremony is a little different," she said. "For one thing, the sun will already be overhead, at its highest point, so I won't have to turn my back on the cove for any length of time." She paused, thinking about it for a moment. "Actually, it could be a little more confrontational than what we did this morning because I'll be out in the open the whole time."

"We'll be there too," John promised. "I'll be right at your side, and the rest of the guys will be backing you up. They can run interference, if needed."

She thought about that for a moment. "A distraction might be helpful if the creature gets too rambunctious. I don't know what it has in store for me tomorrow. It probably didn't expect what we were able to do against it this morning. Tomorrow, it will be better prepared." She frowned. "But I don't want anyone getting too close and putting themselves in too much danger. Is there anything your guys can do from afar that might serve as a distraction?"

John grinned, and it held a tinge of sinister satisfaction. "Zak's an artist with almost any sort of gun. He can take a shot from a mile out and hit what he aims at."

"A sniper?" she asked, surprised.

She knew now that the core group that made up the town council had all been in the military with John, but she hadn't quite realized that some of them had such specialties. She probably should have, she realized. Any shifter soldier would pretty much automatically be one of the best among the best. They couldn't help but stand out with all their shifter advantages when it came to the five senses.

"Do you think bullets will distract the creature?" she asked, wondering out loud.

"Zak tried to shoot one of the smaller ones once before. Regular bullets didn't stop it, but it did notice. It did *bleed*. I'll ask Zak to try hollow points or explosive rounds. Tracer rounds, maybe. I'm not sure what would work best, but Zak will know, and he can try a few different things, all from a safe distance. It might be enough to distract the creature at a crucial moment. What we need to do is work out a system to communicate with Zak outside the circle. You are going to cast another circle, right?"

She nodded. "Yeah. It's safest to be inside wards when battling something so magical. The first thing I'll do is cast the circle, but it'll be a little smaller this time so I can cast it fast. The leviathan will probably be watching me the entire time. I'll need to put up the ward quick, before it can interfere."

"Once that circle is up, it's hard to communicate with anyone outside, right? Does that hold for radio communications?" he asked.

"Probably. I wouldn't want to chance it."

"So we're going to need some sort of visual cue that Zak can see. And we should probably do a test after the excitement is over to see if radio comms work."

She could tell he was making a mental checklist. She liked the way his mind worked. He seemed to see everything in orderly little segments. That had to be at least part of the reason why he'd been so successful in his career, and now in building this amazing town. He attacked a project from many sides at once. She liked that about him...and so much more.

In fact, since she'd been spending more time with him, there was very little she didn't like about the sexy mayor. She'd noticed right away that he was attractive, but now, she knew so much more about him. He drew her, like a moth to a flame—and probably just as dangerous too. But she was powerless to resist his allure.

He also confused the hell out of her. Things had been moving way too fast for the past two days. She felt like she was on a roller-coaster—both exhilarated and scared to death at different points along the way. With any luck, the ride would end well.

Tomorrow, they would do the noon ceremony, and then, the next day, the sunset ceremony. Then all they'd have to do was the all-important full moon ritual, and things might just start to get back to normal for her—or as close as possible with Mellie preparing to do her part after that.

Maybe then, she could take stock rationally of where this thing with John was heading. If it lasted that long. Frankly, she was afraid that, after her part in protecting the cove was over, he would no longer be interested. Stress had a way of making people react differently than they otherwise would.

She hoped that wasn't the case with John, but how well did she really know him? She knew she could trust him to protect her. In essence, she could trust him with her life, but what about her heart?

Urse was very much afraid that if she gave her heart to the Alpha bear, she would never be the same.

Dinner was amazing, and John realized the Ricoletti sisters, in addition to being powerful witches, were also great cooks. He hadn't had a roast that good since his mother's, and that was saying something.

As they lingered over coffee, the phone rang, and Amelia confirmed that she'd be staying overnight at the bakery tonight. When Ursula hung up the phone, her entire demeanor had changed.

John felt it too. There was something in the air between them. Just knowing they would be alone for the rest of the night—if they chose to spend it together—was creating invisible, but palpable, sparks in the air.

John joined her by the couch in the living room part of the open-concept main area of the apartment. He'd placed his jacket on the arm of the couch and he sat next to it now, knowing he would need to consult some of the papers he'd brought with him but had left in his coat pocket while they enjoyed dinner.

"So where do you want to work from tomorrow?" John asked as she joined him on the couch.

"Well, we'd already settled on the north side of town. I'm just not sure exactly where to set the circle." She seemed to ponder the problem, her gaze turning slightly inward in thought.

John reached into the deep inner pocket of his coat and pulled out the rolled map he'd been working on all day in his office. It was a depiction of the cove and the estimated boundaries of the ward Ursula had put in place earlier that morning, along with other geographic features and the coverage points he'd been toying with most of the afternoon.

"I think our best bet is to work in this area." He pointed to a roughly circular area on the north side of town. "If we manage the same radius as this morning, there should be a little overlap and the apex of the cove will be covered."

"That'll protect the town and all of Main Street where it's closest to the water," she observed, looking closely at the map. "I like it." She turned the map for a better look. "I can work with this." Her voice was low, contemplative, as she studied the map. Suddenly, she looked up to meet his gaze. "Did you do all this?"

"I collated the data. My guys did the actual measurements." He felt his bear preening under her scrutiny.

"This is really great," she said, still holding his gaze. "I've always had to just guess before, or go on my own observations. This is really helpful. Thanks for putting it together."

The moment spun out between them until John edged forward, capturing her lips with his. It started out tentatively. He wasn't sure if she'd welcome his kiss or if she would turn him away. He'd willingly follow her lead, whichever way she chose to go.

Much to his joy, she not only accepted his kiss, she deepened it, moving closer to him on the couch and into his arms. John held her tenderly, his bear tempering its strength so as not to frighten or hurt her in any way.

When he leaned back, she followed him, unwilling to let him end their kiss. Well, he was okay with that. John just tucked her closer in his arms, supporting her as she kissed him like her life depended on it. That's when he realized there was a sort of desperation in her kiss that made him wary.

This time, he held her at arms' length, not letting her luscious lips seduce him into allowing the kiss to continue. Not until he knew what was motivating her.

He wanted her kiss almost as much as he wanted his next breath, but only if it came freely, from her heart. He didn't want her to be with him from a place of fear or desperation.

"Wait a sec," he crooned, trying not to break the mood too much.

"Why?" The single word came out on almost a whine.

"Because I want to make sure you're really with me. That you really want this," he all but growled, his inner bear liking the way she felt against his human form.

"I'm with you, John, and I do want this." Her hand rested over his heart, stroking lightly. "I want you."

His heart skipped a beat. Did she really mean that the way it sounded? Sweet Goddess, he hoped so.

"Are you sure?" he made himself ask. "I'm not an easy man."

"I don't want easy. I want you."

Holy moly. She'd said it again. John counted himself a lucky bastard and pulled her closer into his arms.

"I'm not leaving you tonight. Whether or not we sleep

together, I'm going to stay in this apartment. I have to keep you safe, and I don't like the idea of you being all alone up here with your sister staying at the bakery. But I'll stay to protect you, even if we don't end up in bed together."

"But what if I want you in my bed?" Her voice dropped low, into places that made him want to lick her like a honeycomb.

He stood from the couch, with her still in his arms and turned toward the hall that led to her bedroom. "Then you're going to get what you want."

Urse's head spun as John lifted her up off the couch in one fell swoop. The man was just so darn strong. That bear thing was super attractive, if she was being honest with herself.

And that's what it was, really. She was finally being honest about what she wanted. She wanted him.

Everything could all go to hell tomorrow. Nothing about what she planned to do was guaranteed. The leviathan knew about her now and wouldn't be taken by surprise again. It would be waiting for her. Ready.

She could easily die tomorrow, or be gravely injured. She could burn out magically. She could burn out her brain. There were so many dire possibilities that John didn't know about. Being a *strega* wasn't like being a shifter. At least not as far as she had been able to tell. He was merged with his beast. It was part of him and had been since birth.

Her magic was something apart that she called and did her best to control and shape. She could lose control of it all too easily. She could push too far and go beyond her abilities. She could go beyond what was possible for her and into realms where she was in mortal danger of her soul all too easily. John didn't know that—at least, she didn't think he realized it— and she wasn't about to tell him.

The less he knew about the danger to her right now, the better. He was too involved in protecting her, and she had the feeling he'd forbid her from doing what she must if he knew the true depth of the dangers she faced.

Yet she had to do what she could for this town and its people. The shifters who lived here were good people just looking for a peaceful existence. They wanted to be happy. The core group of men had been soldiers and had chosen this little patch of earth to settle down and try to create a life for themselves and whatever females they could find to complete their community.

Urse wanted badly to give them that chance. It was a good goal, they had. A pure one. Peace and love were two objectives she could get behind and endorse.

Maybe that made her a bit of a hippie, she thought with some amusement. She had grown up in San Francisco, after all.

She smiled to herself as John carried her into her bedroom, and then, the amusement changed to a feeling of joy that she was here, in her private sanctum, with this incredible man. She was going to reach for this moment out of time—this night of nights—where they were alone in the apartment and grab it with both hands.

She was going to grab *him* with both hands and hold tight 'til morning.

John let go of her legs, letting her lower body slide down against his until she was standing in front of him, just in front of her bed. She was glad now that she'd opted for a full-size bed when setting up this room, though it would still be a bit too small for a guy of John's height. At least it was better than the twin she'd left behind in her tiny apartment in San Francisco.

He looked downward, meeting her gaze. His eyes were molten with unspoken desires, but there was a tiny bit of reserve that told her he would leave if she gave him the least bit of indication that she didn't want this.

But she wanted it. Oh, how she wanted it.

"You're very tall," she said softly, looking up at him. It was a nonsensical thing to say, but it brought a smile to his lips.

"Is that a complaint?" The gentle amusement in his growly voice told her he wasn't at all serious.

"No. Just an observation," she quipped. "It makes it hard to kiss you unless I do something like this."

She stepped back and up, to stand on the edge of the bed, looking down at him from a few inches. It wasn't much, but it gave her a taste of what it must feel like for him, so far above everyone else's heads all the time.

She looked around, surveying her room with a comical air. "It's kinda nice up here."

"Even nicer down here." He growled in a sexy way, drawing her attention. She realized what he meant as his gaze zeroed in on her breasts, now much closer to his eye level.

"Come here, you," she whispered, cupping the nape of his neck and encouraging his head to tilt upward as hers tilted slightly down.

Yes. There it was. She captured his lips with her own and led him into a kiss that spoke of want and need and...things she didn't dare name this early into their relationship.

After a few minutes of enjoyable friction as their tongues dueled and danced together, she stepped backward on the bed, drawing him onto it. He knelt, putting one arm around her waist and one behind her knees. He helped her come down onto the bed, his strong hands guiding her into just the position he wanted.

She ended up lying on her back while he leaned over her from the side. Looking up at him, she was fascinated by the swirling magic in his eyes. She could actually see it. She could see the bear magic that lurked within his soul. It was beautiful. Like him.

Though she was pretty sure he wouldn't appreciate being called beautiful. Most men were touchy about a word like that. She smiled, thinking of his reaction, tracing the laugh lines around his magical eyes.

"What?" he asked, pausing in their passion as he met her gaze.

She liked that about him. He wasn't an impatient man. In

fact, he seemed to have patience like the mountains around them. Timeless. Ageless. Meaningful.

"I can see the magic swirling in your eyes," she admitted, smiling softly. Let him make of that what he would.

"They say bears have more magic than most shifters," he said, surprising her.

"That's what Nonna taught us. She was proud of the bear in the family tree, even if it didn't pass down to us."

"As she should be," he agreed with a mock modest face. Then he kissed her. Just light, little nibbly kisses on her face and throat. "You taste like honey, Urse."

"Then it's true what they say about bears liking honey?" she teased as he nibbled his way down the sensitive column of her throat.

"Oh, I don't just *like* honey. I *love* honey." He nipped and sucked a particularly responsive spot on her neck, down in the bend by her collarbone. Urse had to bite back a whimper.

Then his fingers were on her clothing, unbuttoning buttons, unzipping zippers, and unhooking hooks. She was all for getting rid of the fabric that separated them. She pushed at his shoulders, wanting his shirt off. She didn't care where it went or how. She just wanted it gone.

Once again she wished she was more like that old time witch on TV, and could make things disappear with a wiggle of her nose, but sadly, magic didn't work that way. At least, hers didn't. Instead, she tugged at the hem of his shirt, pulling it out of his pants while he worked on her clothing.

She probably hindered more than helped, but her foggy mind didn't quite realize it. Never before had she been so eager to share pleasure that she almost stopped thinking altogether and just...felt.

John did that. Only him. He overpowered her conscious mind and sent her into a realm where only sensation mattered. The scents, sounds and feel of him against her were the only things that registered. Thoughts of the past and future were banished, and all that existed was the now. A delicious now that included a hunky grizzly shifter in man form, who knew exactly how to drive her wild.

CHAPTER NINE

John did his best to hold in the growl of his bear as he shed his clothing and helped Ursula out of hers. The bear was very much present in his mind as he made preparations to join with her for the first time.

That was new.

Never before had his bear side taken much notice of the women he fucked. Sure, it pushed him to take pleasure where he found it, but it hadn't been interested in the women themselves, only in the end result. This time was different. This time, the bear side was well aware of the magical woman beneath its alternate form, and it was encouraging John's human side to take her and make her theirs.

The bear was thinking *mate*. John had thought about that for the past day or two, and had come to terms with the concept, though neither his human side nor his bear side would know for sure until they had claimed her. It might've been different had she also been a shifter, but Ursula had only the faintest traces of shifter blood in her ancestry, and John had no idea if she felt the mating pull as strongly as he did.

Time would tell. Time, and actually being inside her, learning her body and touching her soul. Only then would both halves of his nature be satisfied and know for certain whether or not she was the one woman destined for him.

He had a strong suspicion that she was, though. This was probably just going to confirm it, and Lady help them both when he knew for sure.

It would change everything. Both for the better and possibly for the worse, if his people couldn't accept their mating and he had to give up everything he'd worked for here. He would, though it wouldn't be easy, but his true mate would be worth it. If that's what she was.

And he was about to find out.

He'd wanted to take his time undressing her, but it was impossible. Not this first time. Maybe…after he'd taken the edge off…in a few years, maybe…he'd be able to take his time with her. But for right now, the passion was rising and driving him hard. Luckily, she was with him. The way she tugged at his shoulders and sank her flat, human teeth into his lip—not to hurt, but to encourage—told him that she was as eager as him.

Within moments, they were both naked, and heaven help him if he broke her flimsy little bed. He supposed it was what regular folk called a *double* bed, but it wasn't anywhere near big enough for him, much less both of them. Hell, if he managed to break the thing, he'd just have an excuse to make her a real bed, out of sturdy pine, and big enough to hold them both and more importantly—hold *up* to anything they might get up to in it.

The thought made him grin. He liked the idea of making a bed especially for them. A little love nest. A place only they would ever use.

But he was getting a little ahead of himself. Again. *Dammit.*

He tried to slow himself down and really appreciate the moment, but it was hard. Actually, *he* was too hard to go slow, but he owed it to Ursula to give her more to remember than a blur from their first time together.

He made himself look at her. Her luscious curves made his mouth water, and without conscious thought, he began to work his way down her neck, over her collarbones and onto her chest. His hands sought out the soft weight of her full breasts, offering them up for his lips, tongue and the gentle pressure of his teeth. He was careful of her delicate skin, but he knew she liked what he was doing when she shivered in his arms and moaned in delight.

He could really get used to hearing that sound. *Damn.* That made his dick even harder, which was something he'd thought impossible only moments before.

Her skin tasted like honey, and her scent was that of the cool, green grass of a spring meadow. Fresh. Pure. Magical. Little sparks of her energy zinged him gently, adding a sparkle of sensation everywhere they touched. It wasn't unpleasant. In fact, it was almost addictive. The tingle made him feel more alive and brought a certain amount of joy to the proceedings, which was a new one for him. Her magic sparked against his in a happy way that he felt right down to the soles of his feet. Interesting.

John ran his hands down over her ribs, framing her waist, which made her squirm a bit.

"Ticklish?" he asked, raising up enough to meet her gaze. Her cheeks were flushed with arousal…and perhaps a bit of shyness?

"A little, I guess." She looked uncomfortable admitting to it, so he didn't tease her. Why would a woman as beautiful as Ursula not be used to men touching her waist? Maybe there hadn't been that many before him? Maybe she was shy about her body?

She had nothing to be shy about. Ursula was built solid. Bombshell solid. Nicely rounded hips, generous breasts. Maybe she wasn't the waif-thin skeleton many humans aimed for nowadays, but John didn't want a scarecrow. He wanted a woman. Specifically, he wanted *this* woman. The way she was put together only drew him more, if he were being honest. He liked the way she looked, and he'd spend some time convincing her of that little detail as they got to know each other better.

At the same time, he had a primitive sort of moment

thinking that she hadn't let too many other men touch her like this. He wanted to growl in satisfaction. Not that he'd begrudge her anything in her past, but he was just possessive enough to want to be the one to show her all the delights he knew they would find together. He liked that it would be new to her. Or at least, not old hat. If that made him a bit of a caveman, then so be it.

"Don't worry, honey," he whispered, moving his lips back into contact with her skin, pausing to dip his tongue into her navel. "I've got you." He reveled in the shivers that overtook her body as he worshiped her with his mouth.

He had more in store, but he'd have to move this along if he wanted to keep from embarrassing himself. When he came, he wanted to be inside her, not jetting into the sheets like some untried kid.

Urse couldn't believe the way John was making her feel. She'd been with a few guys, but every encounter with John so far had been something completely new in her experience, and tonight was no exception. She was glad he wasn't teasing her about being ticklish. She couldn't help it. She wasn't really used to people touching her body so intimately, so she was still a bit more sensitive than she probably should be at her age.

So sue me.

But John seemed to understand. Rather than double down on the teasing and making her super uncomfortable, he simply went on touching her gently, careful of her more sensitive areas. He kept the mood going flawlessly, without triggering her embarrassment in any way. He was a gem, and he made her feel cherished.

That was new. Exciting. Enticing. She'd never felt so special in a man's arms before. She'd never felt like the man she was with wanted to be with *her*—and not just a willing female body. With John, she was sure he knew exactly who he was with and that he'd made the deliberate choice to be with her, even though his people might object.

She didn't like the idea that he might get into trouble with his Clan over this, but by the same token, she was powerless to deny the attraction between them. It was bigger than Clan politics. Bigger than societal prohibitions. Bigger than the two of them combined.

It felt...important. And necessary.

She'd figure out what that might mean later, but for now, she was just going to enjoy the moment. Their one night together that might be all they were allowed. If that were the case, then by the Lady, she was going to enjoy these stolen hours with everything that was in her.

She squealed a bit when John's hands slid between her thighs and pressed outward, presenting her most private place to his gaze. She looked down and saw the way he was gazing at her, studying her body. He licked his lips, and she shivered in anticipation.

Was he going to...? Sweet Mother in heaven!

Urse's hips came off the bed when John's mouth covered her clit. And when his tongue roved downward and inward... *Holy moly!*

His hands framed her hips, holding her, guiding her. His mouth remained fastened below, his talented tongue teasing and licking, flicking and pressing. She nearly swooned as she came under his ministrations, crying out his name as her hips bucked in his hands.

He rode her through the small orgasm, gentling her with his strong hands, rekindling the flames of her arousal when she'd really thought she'd need some kind of break. But there were no breaks. Not with John still so ready, so hard and obviously eager to join with her. And she found, after only a few moments, she was just as eager. She wanted to know what he would feel like inside her, claiming her, possessing her.

She wanted it with all her heart.

And then, he moved over her, slotting his big body between her legs and holding his chest just a few inches above hers. He was leaning on his elbows, careful not to crush her, but the way she was feeling, she wanted to know what his weight would feel like against her body, covering her completely.

He was big though. Built on the massive side, even for a shifter. So she'd follow his lead and let him decide what she could handle, for now. She didn't want any sort of disagreement—even a silly one—to interfere with this first joining. She trusted him to take care of her, which felt like something his beast half would truly appreciate.

She'd ask him about it later, if they could somehow make this work long enough to actually have a *later*. For now, she was just going to go with the flow and live in the moment, trusting John's protective instincts to see them both safely through to the end.

Had she ever trusted a man this much before? Sadly, she realized she hadn't. No one had ever been like John. Quite possibly, no one ever would again.

When he pushed inward, claiming her with his thick cock, she held her breath. He went slow, letting her body become accustomed to his size, but when she figured she'd taken all she could, he kept pushing. Surprisingly, her body accepted more than she'd thought she could. There was no pain, only the slight, scintillating burn of her body stretching to take in something of a size it had never had before.

Long, thick, hard. John was amazing.

He began to move. Just a rocking motion, at first, while her body got used to him. He rubbed up against her clit on each push inward, and she was soon clutching at his shoulders, begging him silently to go faster, to push deeper.

And then, he did. She met him thrust for thrust, both of their bodies moving in time. Her fingers wrapped around his shoulders, and she felt the fine edge of control in his muscles as he strained against her. Faster, he plunged, and she heard a rhythmic moaning sound coming from somewhere. It took a moment before she realized it was coming from her. She was moaning in time with his thrusts.

When the pleasure swept her up and cast her among the

stars, she screamed his name, pouring out her rapture to the heavens. She felt John's body tighten within her, joining her in ecstasy.

It was perfect.

And it was devastating.

Why would the Mother Goddess let her touch such perfection on earth, if she wasn't meant to be with him? Would the Lady be so cruel? Or would some solution to their little magic problem show itself and allow them to be together?

Urse didn't know what to think. All she could do for now was hold on tight...for the rest of their stolen night.

*

At the appointed hour the next day, Urse cast her circle on the other side of town. As before, John was at her side and stayed in the circle with her while she worked. Unlike the day before, she now knew what it was to be with him, and that knowledge flowed through her every action. Just standing next to him as she worked seemed somehow more intimate now.

Everything about being around him was both more comfortable and somewhat exciting. Even the most innocent touch made sparks run up and down her spine. Sparks of magic? Or sparks of desire? And with him—unlike any other man she'd ever gotten close to—were they one and the same?

He was so intensely magical it almost took her breath away. His magic shone through in everything he did, now that she knew it so intimately. His magic made her feel warm, and it sparkled against hers in a joyful way.

The casting of the circle went a lot faster due both to the smaller size of the circle and the easy cooperation between herself and John. He knew what to expect this time and was ready to help her even before she knew she needed help.

When the sun hit the highest point in the sky and was at its strongest, she cast her magic. As before, John had added his own flavor of magic to her spell, and she thought the blending of energies made her spell stronger. It added shifter magic to her wards that would, in all likelihood, make the protections easier for the shifters to deal with. Knowing how magical bear shifters were now, Urse had realized that many of the bears would probably feel the tingle of the wards as they went about their business.

It probably wouldn't bother anybody, but the added dimension of John's shifter magic would make it easier—more comfortable—for the shifters who might notice it. That was probably an important thing to consider in a town full of shifters.

When she released the spell, the leviathan put up a show of thrashing around as it was pushed back from the part of the cove she'd just managed to ward, but it wasn't quite like what had happened yesterday. Urse wasn't going to complain, but it definitely made her wonder. The smaller creatures acted about the same, but the big kahuna wasn't fighting the way she'd expected.

Nevertheless, she saw the spell through to the end. The ward set, and Urse broke the circle, lowering the shield between John and her and the rest of the world.

John touched her shoulder, drawing her attention. She turned to him, meeting the concerned look on his face with one of her own.

"Did that seem just a little too easy?" he asked quietly.

She squinted up at him. "I didn't want to say it, but…"

"Yeah." John put his arm around her shoulders, and just the warmth of that move made her feel better. "Let's check with my guys. They were watching too, and they'll be scouting to test the results of this afternoon's work."

She walked with him toward the small gathering of men, which included the sheriff, Brody, his deputy, Zak, and Peter. All three of them looked skeptical, which meant they'd realized something was a little different too. Urse's heart sank.

Urse and John joined the threesome, and they all seemed to wait for John to speak. Even Urse was waiting for the

Alpha, which struck her as a little funny.

"I can tell by the looks on your faces that you saw what we did," John began. "We need to check why that critter was so damned cocky today."

"The spell set as it should. I could feel it," Urse put in.

"Early reports say it took effect just like yesterday, but we'll do more testing, of course," Brody said, lifting his walkie-talkie. "At least we were able to verify that electronic comms don't work inside the circle."

Urse hadn't realized it, but apparently, John and his men had been trying to communicate over the radio headset John had worn. She wasn't surprised it hadn't worked. Magic had a tendency to interfere with mundane things every once in a while.

"We have our work cut out for us then," John said quietly, eyeing each of the men who reported to him. They started discussing logistics and who was stationed where and doing what.

Urse felt herself drooping. The energy output had been the same as the day before. It was a little easier to handle but still incredibly tiring. Urse just wanted to get horizontal and unconscious for a few hours, until her energy had a chance to regenerate.

"I'm going to head back to the bookstore," she put in when there was a break in the conversation. She stifled a yawn. "The whole area near Main Street should be safe now. I'm not sure where the ward ends. You'll be able to tell me that after you do your tests," she said, gesturing toward the men. "Be careful. That creature is up to something. I have no idea what, but be on the lookout for anything strange."

"Good advice," John seconded as her voice trailed off into another yawn she couldn't quite hold back. He then turned to her. "Do you need help getting back to the store?"

"No, I'm fine. Like I said, this area is warded. I'll be okay from here to the bookstore. It's not that far, and Mellie's waiting there for me. I'm going to sleep for a few hours." She reached up without thinking to kiss John's cheek before turning to walk away.

Only then did she realize what she'd done when she saw the raised eyebrows on the sheriff, deputy and their friend Peter. *Oops.*

She'd just outed their change in relationship. Maybe. Urse had a hard time finding the energy to care. She would apologize to John later, in case he hadn't wanted anyone to know about them yet. And of course, she'd have to come clean with Mellie sooner rather than later.

But she'd talk with Mel after she took a nice long nap. Frankly, she didn't have the energy to do much more than go to the store, fumble her way upstairs and find her bed.

Ursula had kissed him. In public. Just a peck on the cheek, but it was so out of character for him and the women he dealt with day to day, every one of the guys noticed.

"So…you and the *strega*, eh boss?" Peter said with a speculative gleam in his eye. "Nice." The approving nod that accompanied his words surprised John.

"Really?" John would have squeaked, if his basso profundo voice had been capable of making such a sound.

"Hell yeah, man," Zak said casually. "She's a pretty gal, and her magic is pure. If you could see it the way I do…" Zak trailed off, and John saw the way his gaze unfocused.

"Golden sparks and healthy green swirls?" John supplied, wondering if the only one of his men who could actually perceive magic with his eyes saw the same thing John did when he was standing inside the magic circle with Ursula.

Zak's gaze snapped back to John. "Yeah. That's exactly what it looks like. Pure gold, which is one of the highest forms of energy, and healthy green, which means growth and nurturing. That's a heady combination." Zak nodded, giving his own approval. "She's the real deal, *mon ami*. Her wards are permanent, and mixed with your strong Alpha magic, they'll protect this town and its shifters forever. That's some powerful mojo. She's good people."

John was thrilled by the response, but Brody hadn't said

anything. Zak was one of his most trusted men, as was Peter, but Brody was his second in command. His opinion held a little more weight than the others.

"And you?" John asked Brody directly, wanting to get it over with. If Brody didn't like the idea that the Alpha was getting involved with a magic user, his opinion would hold a lot of weight with the rest of the guys. "What do you think?"

Brody held his gaze and stood casually, but John knew he was fully alert, as he always was. Brody was a soldier's soldier, as were most of his men, but Brody was the XO, the one who could be relied on to act when and if the Alpha wasn't around. Next to John, Brody was the default leader of this powerful group of fighting shifters.

"Are you serious about her?" Brody asked quietly, not giving anything away.

John hadn't expected to have to come clean this way, but maybe it was best to get it over with, so he knew where he stood. So be it.

"Yeah. I think she's my mate." There. He'd said it out loud. *Whew.*

Brody made him wait for a heartbeat more, then his face split in a grin. "Well, hot damn. I can't say I ever expected we'd have magic users in this town, but if it's the Ricoletti sisters, then it's okay with me. Both of those gals are on the right side, and they wouldn't intentionally hurt a fly. My mate and her sisters love those girls, and I think they'll squeal in happiness when they realize you've been snared by one."

Brody went one step further and stuck out his hand. John took it and received not only a shake, but a manly bro hug and a few pounding slaps on his back. The gesture was repeated by Zak and then Peter, in turn.

John was floored. He hadn't expected to get such an easy pass from his guys. He thought at least some would object to the idea of allowing the witches to not only stay in town, but for one to become mate of the Alpha. Of course, this was only three of the group, but they were an important three. Judging by their reactions, the rest of the group might not be so bad.

"I already decided I'd step down as Alpha if I had to. A true mate is more important than anything else. If we have to leave town, I'll do that too," he revealed, glad of the immediate denial he could see in his friends' faces.

"I don't think there'll be any need for that," Brody said quietly. "Everybody can see what Ursula is doing here, and how much she's giving of herself to do it. If that doesn't earn her a place in our hearts, and in our community, then I don't know what else would."

John felt his heart warm as he realized that his guys hadn't disappointed him. He'd been willing to give up his dream of this town for the dream of a true mate, but now, it looked like he might just have a shot at having it all. His town and his mate. The best of both worlds.

John's warm and fuzzy feelings were cut short as his cell phone rang. He removed the small device from his belt and looked at the number. It was Amelia's cell number. John frowned and pushed the button to answer.

"Hello?"

"John, is Urse still with you?" Amelia sounded worried.

"No." John frowned. "She left a few minutes ago. She should be at the bookstore by now." John started looking toward the street where Ursula had disappeared. A few hand signals had the other guys looking as well.

"She's not here, and I can't get out. The damn ward is still up, and she has to be the one to set me free. John, I'm worried. She wouldn't have had much energy left after casting that spell. She should've come home to sleep it off."

"That's what she said she was going to do," John agreed, even as he began searching the street. "I'm on it. I'll find her. Sit tight. I'll phone when we have her."

"Find her fast, John. She's in no state to be out on her own right now when her energy is so low."

John ended the call, cursing himself for not going with Ursula. He should have seen her safely back to the bookstore. *Dammit!*

Brody came up to him, waiting to hear what John would say.

"Ursula is missing. She didn't make it back to the bookstore, and she locked her sister in magically. Amelia can't come out until the wards come down, so she can't help. I'm going bear to see if I can sniff her out." John was already stripping, handing his wallet and electronic gear to Brody. "Put everyone on alert. Keep checking the extent of the ward she put up today and make notes, but have everyone keep an eye out for Ursula. She couldn't have gotten far."

Brody nodded, putting all of John's stuff into a net bag that had been in one of his cargo pockets. They walked into an alley as John stripped completely bare. He left his clothes for Brody to take care of and shifted quickly to his grizzly form.

CHAPTER TEN

Where was that singing coming from? Urse stumbled a bit on her way back to the bookstore as an eerily discordant melody flowed through her from all over. Or was it coming from over there?

Urse followed the tones of the song, wanting to know more. She was at her lowest ebb of energy and perhaps not thinking too clearly, but something made her follow the siren song she heard with every fiber of her being. It was alluring. *Luring.*

Something was wrong.

No. The song was calling her.

Urse left the sidewalk and went up one of the alleys between buildings. There wasn't much to Main Street. Just a strip of galleries and stores, some with alleys that led to the back. Behind that, only the woods. Thick woods. Pines and mysterious Pacific Northwest growth. A few mighty redwoods were found deeper into the forest, but Douglas fir and more common pines populated the area behind Main Street.

Urse found herself walking into the forest, following the song as it pulled her to the left, through the thick undergrowth and around the edge of the cove, hidden in the woods. The pitch of the song changed, and she followed it, yawning, but unable to break away.

Her feet dragged through the undergrowth, and she was vaguely aware of her skin being scratched by branches and brambles, but she didn't really feel it. She didn't feel much of anything. The song was all-consuming.

It drove her. Dragged her. Gave her just enough energy to pull her tired body through the forest.

Something was wrong.

No. The song was all important.

No. Something was wrong.

Her consciousness rose as her steps faltered. The song raged louder, calling her even more vehemently.

That wasn't right. Her head cleared a little as the wrongness of her actions penetrated the fog around her mind.

She stopped walking but found she couldn't move away. She could only go forward. Her feet were frozen if she tried to move back the way she'd come.

Oh, yeah. That was definitely wrong.

Her head cleared more as panic set in. She couldn't move. Now *that* was a problem.

And magically, she was at her lowest point. Her internal energies would need time to regenerate. The song still sang in her ears, but she recognized it now. It was a siren song, though she doubted any sea siren was at the root of it. No, this was the leviathan singing in its inhuman, magical voice, luring her to come to it so it could destroy her.

Panic was a mild word for what she was feeling.

She strove for calm. And she began to pray. She prayed as she had never prayed before, asking for the Mother of All to send help and if not help, then a quick and painless end.

A throaty growl sounded from behind her along with the sounds of a big body crashing through the undergrowth. It had to be a bear, but was it a regular ol' bear or one of the shifters? And if it was a shifter—which was likely—who was it? Was it someone who would help her? Or was it someone who really hated magic users and would rather see her gone?

A tear worked its way past her eye and down her cheek as

she waited to learn her fate.

John whuffed a sigh of relief when he found Ursula standing in the forest. But something was still wrong. She wasn't moving. He approached cautiously.

He'd followed her trail easily enough. She hadn't tried to hide her steps. It had been a puzzling trail though. She sort of meandered through the woods until she turned sharply toward the cove, following a parallel path northward around the upper arc of the cove itself.

She had stopped at the point where she was turning toward the water. Her parallel path had brought her around the cove to an area that wasn't covered by the ward of protections she'd cast today and yesterday. If she approached the beach here, the leviathan and its minions could still get to her.

What was she doing? She had stopped, so if the leviathan's evil magic was drawing her in, she was fighting it. She looked frozen in place, unable to move.

He growled a question, wondering if she'd understand.

"Whoever you are, I can't move. So either be merciful and end me fast, or come over here and show yourself." Her voice shook with emotion, but he admired the way she was standing tall, facing her fate.

He walked up to her on all fours, placing himself in front of her. Would she recognize him in this form?

"John?" Her voice was tentative, but a thread of relief sounded through her tone. He sat on his haunches, trying to look non-threatening. "John, that is you, isn't it?" He nodded his bear-shaped head, and she sighed in relief. "Thank the Lady."

He shifted, flowing from his bear into his human form. He might be naked and unarmed, but he figured she needed his words of reassurance more than anything else right now. And he was a strong enough bear that he could shift back into his more lethal form—or the most dangerous form of all, the half-shift battle form—in the blink of an eye.

"Are you all right?" He wanted desperately to take her in his arms, but he wasn't sure if that would cause more problems right now. Whatever was holding her in place, it had to be magic, and she was the resident expert on that stuff.

She solved his dilemma by launching herself into his arms. He caught her with a small *oof* of expelled air as she hit him, but his arms went around her and held tight.

"I couldn't break its spell, but your shift—the shifter magic interceded and cut the cord that tied me to the leviathan. Thank the Lady you came along when you did." She was speaking rapid fire, near panicked as she hugged him tight and placed little kisses of relief all along the side of his face. "I don't know if I could have held out for much longer."

He drew back to look downward, meeting her gaze. "You were fighting it. I could see that. You would have prevailed. You're stronger than it, honey. You're the strongest woman I know."

He gave in to impulse and kissed her lips, keeping it short because they were standing in the middle of the forest and the leviathan was still out there. Who knew what other tricks it had up its...uh...tentacles?

"We're not too far from my place," he whispered as he ended the kiss. "Are you okay now? Free of it—whatever it was—completely?"

She nodded. "Yeah. You broke the spell when you shifted right in front of me. Your magic must've short circuited the connection."

"Come on then. Let's go home." He turned her, keeping one arm over her shoulders and headed off through the woods.

The house was two stories built into the side of the hill, overlooking the cove. It was high enough that it was well away from the water, and they'd had to climb quite a ways uphill to get to it. Inside John's mind, his bear was doing mental cartwheels in joy that he was bringing her to its den.

John tried to be a little more circumspect...though being naked for the journey through the forest on two feet wasn't exactly *circumspect*.

When they were still about twenty yards out from the house, John stopped suddenly. He smelled something. It was like ozone and unearthly flowers. He'd scented it before. Just once.

"I'm going bear. Whatever happens, stay behind me."

"What is it?" He knew he was scaring her, but he couldn't help it.

"No time. Stay behind..." His words faded into a low growl as he went down onto all fours. His shoulder was about the same height as hers, which meant his bear was big enough to shield her, should it become necessary. He hoped it wouldn't be necessary.

He approached the house slowly. There was a deck off the side of the house, and that was his angle of approach. The door there would be accessible. It had an electronic combo lock, which would work even when he was naked and had no keys.

He paced slowly forward, growling low until he could see the stranger sitting on the wooden steps that led up to the deck. And what he saw made him sit back on his haunches in sheer surprise.

With Ursula's hand on his shoulder, the vision in front of him was enhanced. It took the shape of a man...

A man in glowing armor, a shining sword held point down, its tip touching the earth as the knight's hands rested on the pommel. His head hung down, but it rose as John went silent in shock.

"I mean ye no harm, laddie. I am here to learn what strange magics are in play in this hidden cove of yours, and as I believe is proper among your people, I come to the Alpha first, to make my presence known." He bowed his head again, holding John's gaze, and then, his focus went to Ursula. "And I came now because of your prayers, lass. The Lady sent me, but I see your grizzly friend has already rescued you."

"Are you a…a knight, sir? A Knight of the Light?" Ursula whispered from behind John's furry ear.

"Is that how you see me?" The man gave them a lopsided smile.

John noted how the sword point sent out tendrils of pure golden energy into the earth. It was welcomed by the land around his home, as if it was a blessing. And it felt that way to John too. This guy was something out of John's realm of experience, but he knew that scent…

"Armor, glowing sword…" Ursula whispered.

And just like that, the glowing image winked out, leaving the same man dressed in jeans and a leather bomber jacket. The sword was gone, though the man's elbows still rested on his knees, his hands held together in front of him, where the sword hilt had been. John blinked. Then he growled.

The man's hands rose, palms outward in a gesture of calm. "Be at ease, my friend. You were seeing something few are ever granted leave to see. I don't really know why, but I suspect it has to do with the magic you've both been exposed to in recent hours. I've come to learn what passes here on behalf of Others who would be allies with those on the side of Light."

"I think I speak for John when I say, we can use all the allies we can get. The leviathan almost got me just now, and I still have two more rituals to perform before my magic is maxed out here."

"Then you are the lady mage among these shifters," the stranger said, rising to his feet and coming down the steps to stand in front of them.

John got back on his feet, ready to defend Ursula, should it be necessary. He wanted to talk to this guy, but he also couldn't shift into his naked, vulnerable human form with an unknown quantity like the glowing knight/bomber jacket guy so close. John growled in frustration.

"Who are you?" Ursula asked instead of confirming the man's suspicions. *Good girl.*

"Forgive me." The man gave a charming smile. "My name

is Cameron. Perhaps I should go stand over there for a bit while the Alpha has a chance to shift and dress so we can talk." He stepped back, giving John and Ursula a wide berth, letting John pivot to keep the guy in sight while he moved away from the house.

John didn't hesitate. He nudged Ursula up the steps and toward the door, sniffing for all he was worth. Nothing had been tampered with on the deck or near the house. Cameron had only been sitting on the steps and before that...? John had no idea. There was no other trace of scent, but then again, maybe he'd missed it on the way to the steps. He'd check again later, but for now, he wanted to get his clothes and his weapons. Not necessarily in that order.

John hit the combo with one carefully placed claw, keeping Ursula behind him, John's body a shield between her and the stranger. The door popped open, and he urged her to enter, kicking the door shut behind him with his hind foot.

John shifted as he walked, grabbing spare clothes he'd left over the couch when he'd sorted his laundry a few days ago. The housekeeping duties had taken a backseat lately, which turned out to be a good thing right now.

"What do you think?" Ursula asked in a low voice as he moved around inside.

John grabbed a spare handgun from its hidden compartment in the ottoman and tucked it into the spot at the small of his back where it belonged.

"I'm not sure what to think at this point, but I know that scent. That guy is more magical than you and I put together."

"He's a knight," she said, as if he was supposed to recognize what she meant.

"What kind of knight? And why should I trust that means he's on our side in all this?" John asked as he peeked out the window to see the stranger still standing at the edge of the deck, his hands in his pockets.

"Haven't you ever heard of the *Chevalier de la Lumiere?* Knights of the Light? They're the ultra good guys. They are chosen by the Mother of All to serve Her directly. They are rare and good through and through. They fight evil and answer pleas for help on behalf of the Goddess." Ursula made a sound of surprise, and when John looked over at her, one hand was covering her mouth and her eyes were wide. "I prayed, John." She met his gaze, blinking. "I prayed to the Lady. And then, he showed up…" She turned to look out the window.

John was suspicious. "Could be a coincidence," he offered, watching her reaction carefully.

"I don't think it was," she said slowly, her gaze going from the man in the backyard back to John. "I think he came here because I asked the Lady for help."

Ursula's eyes closed as she clasped her hands together, seeming to direct a quick prayer heavenward. Perhaps it was a prayer of thanks, John thought, impressed with her piety but still very suspicious of the newcomer.

It was time to figure out what was going on with the guy. Cameron. And that brogue? What was that all about?

"Will you do me a favor and stay inside, just until I know what we're up against?" John asked her.

Ursula regarded him with a serious gaze. "I'll stand by, but for the record, I think he's okay. I think he was sent."

"Let me just try to make sure, okay?" John hugged her close for just a moment, placing a quick kiss on the top of her head.

"Okay. I bow to the Alpha. You've got your Clan to think about, and I suppose it's only right that you're cautious." She kissed him on the cheek and stepped back.

John went out to meet the stranger, all his senses on alert.

"You're fey," he said before Cameron could speak. John hoped to put the other man on the defensive by going on offense, but it didn't quite work out that way.

"Aye," Cameron admitted freely, which was something John hadn't quite expected. "Fey and sworn to the service of the Lady since the last time the Destroyer walked in this realm." He nodded as if he felt the weight of every one of those many years. Centuries. "Sharp of you to notice. Ye've met my kind before then?"

"Once," was all John would say on the matter. His last run-in with a fey wasn't something he liked to talk about. "That one encounter left me with a bad impression." John scowled, but it didn't seem to affect Cameron.

"Sorry to hear that, laddie. I truly am, but as in all races, we have our good eggs and our bad apples. And a whole lot of regular folk just trying to live their lives in peace, in between."

"Is that what you're doing? Just trying to live your life?" John challenged.

"Och, no. I'm one of those, like you, who fight for those who just want to live in peace. Some of us have to stand up or we all fall, is that not so?"

John had to admit he heard the ring of truth in the fey's words. He'd play along a little further.

"So what brings you here, to my little corner of the world?" John asked, folding his arms casually as he leaned against a tree.

He was aware of movement in the woods. His guys were circling back. He hadn't had time to tell them he'd found Ursula yet, but they were regrouping around him, according to plan. His casual air would tell them to hang back and watch. Frankly, he was glad of the backup at this particular moment. Fey were powerful and could be very unpredictable.

"The magic you've been throwing around up here for the past two days has left ripples through space and time. Permanent wards affect more than just this realm, and aren't ever cast lightly. That you have someone with that kind of power up here has drawn attention," Cameron answered candidly. "The fact that such wards are needing to be cast, and the decidedly other-realm magic being launched by the other side drew even more attention."

"So you figured you'd come up here and stick your nose in? Fey can't resist large quantities of magic and all that?" John sneered, trying to draw a reaction from the guy, but he wasn't playing. So far, so good.

"Actually, I'm friendly with the Master of Napa Valley and the Redstone Clan. I was consulting with them on their little *Venifucus* problem a while back and decided to stick around for a while. California is a lovely place, and the wine Atticus brews is tasty." Cameron smiled. "Marc LaTour—the Master I mentioned—consulted with your friend, Hiram, and learned about the critter problem you have up here. But that still wasn't enough to get me to pop in. I don't just show up. It was your lady who tipped the scales. Her prayer allowed me to travel here to render assistance, but you already had things well in hand, so I decided to retreat to your backyard and wait to introduce myself, as is only proper."

Now that made John think. Cameron certainly seemed to know the right people.

John let out a whistle from between his teeth. It was a low sound, pitched just right to signal one of his team in particular. A moment later, Zak melted from the shadows at John's elbow. To his credit, Cameron didn't flinch.

"Zak, would you mind calling your vampire friend and checking this guy's story?" John asked Zak, holding Cameron's gaze.

"My pleasure, Alpha." Zak stepped a pace or two away and hit speed dial.

Hiram, the Master vampire of the Seattle area, was a new ally and silent partner in Zak's new business venture. Zak had saved the vampire's life when the leviathan had eaten Hiram's yacht for dinner and the bloody, half-dead vampire washed up on shore. Since then, they'd struck up a friendship, and Hiram had become a trusted ally of the Clan.

John watched Cameron as Zak spoke to Hiram. Although it was still afternoon, John knew that some of the really old vamps could move around indoors, though they were usually sluggish.

Hiram was truly ancient. John had tried to discreetly trace Hiram's origins back through the years but had hit a dead end sometime around the middle ages. Hiram was even older than that though, John thought.

Zak hung up after a few more words and nodded at John.

"Hiram confirms his story,"

"Well, that's one point in your favor," John said.

"Oh, come *on*, John. Can't you see he's one of the good guys?" Ursula's exasperated voice came to him from the deck.

"I thought I asked you to stay inside," he said quietly, shaking his head. He wasn't mad though. Actually, he was surprised she'd stayed inside this long.

"'Tis all right, lass. Your Alpha carries a great weight of responsibility for his people. He has to be sure," the fey said, surprising John.

"Well, sir knight, *I'm* sure about you. Thank you for coming to my aid, even if it turned out to be unnecessary at that time. I could use some advice on how to handle my next two planned encounters with the leviathan, if you're willing to discuss it."

"It would be my honor, and please, call me Cam." He winked at her, and John felt a twist in his gut. Why was that sly old fey winking at his girl?

"Cam, it is. And I'm Urse." She smiled at the fey, and John felt his hackles rise. This was getting out of hand.

The bear urged him to take control of the situation, preferably by planting a fist in Cam's smiling mug. Luckily, John's human side was in charge right now, though he was sorely tempted to follow the bear's instincts. Still, if this guy could be an ally in the fight against the leviathan and help keep Ursula safe, then John had to be cautious about offending the guy. *Dammit.*

"Might as well join us on the deck," John invited none too graciously. "Zak, gather the guys and set a perimeter watch. Two-minute check-ins. I don't want anybody else being lured by that sea monster. Ask Brody and Tom to join us on the deck asap."

"Roger that," Zak said shortly, fading into the trees and reaching for the radio attached to his collar.

John escorted the fey up the couple of steps to the deck. There was a table and chairs there, beside the covered grill.

Ursula sat first, followed by the fey as John watched, and then, finally, John took a seat. There were two empty seats between Ursula and Cameron for Brody and Tom, when they got there. That way, there would be two trusted bears between her and the fey on one side, and John on the other. His bear growled in approval.

Ursula had already launched into a discussion of magic with the fey that had John a little lost, but it didn't matter. She understood what Cam was saying, and that was enough. If it would help protect her tomorrow, so much the better.

Brody and Tom arrived together, coming in from the woods. They each stopped to greet Cam, shaking hands with the fey, who stood to greet them, before everyone sat down again.

"I've heard about this town, you know," Cam said, surprising them all. "One of the Redstones mentioned the experiment you were undertaking up here, and he speculated on whether or not a bunch of bears could make a go of living together in one place. The cats have a hard enough time of it, apparently." Cam chuckled, but John heard the hint of a question in his words.

"We're making it work," he said noncommittally.

"Redstones are mostly cougars, right?" Brody asked. "I crossed paths with Steve Redstone early on in my military career."

"The Redstone family itself is cougar," Cam confirmed. "But their Clan, as I'm sure you know, encompasses many other species. They have a number of wolf Packs under their umbrella as well as more than a few solitary bears and entire fighting wings of raptors. They all come under the Clan banner and work for the Redstone Construction company. I thought maybe they'd done some work for you up here in building the town."

John wasn't giving out information here. He didn't really know this guy, though he was willing to give him the benefit of the doubt for now. Still, Cam wasn't going to be learning much from them tonight. No, the information flow would have to be going the other way for now. Until they were sure about him.

"We do a lot of our own work," Tom said, politely ending that line of conversation. Tom was the town lawyer and even more cautious in his words than John.

Cam merely nodded and moved on. "As to your leviathan problem...how do you actually know it is a leviathan, and not some other beastie from the deep?"

"My Nonna has connections," Ursula volunteered. "The *strega* in Italy have been talking about the return of the leviathan for months now. And recently, some have been talking about the return of the Destroyer as if it has already happened."

Cam's mouth tightened into a grim line. "I pray they're wrong," he said. "I fought that she devil once before." If possible, his expression grew even more troubled. "It wasna easy to banish her the first time. Many good people were killed in the effort. Believe me when I tell you, nobody wants to go through that again."

"We believe it," Tom said quietly.

"But if *strega* have seen it..." Cam's head shook. "Well, that's not good. Most *strega* are on our side. Those left in the old country are aligned with the church there—however they work that with their conflicting beliefs—and the side of Light."

"The beliefs aren't as conflicting as you might think," Ursula said with a small smile. "Nonna makes it work, and she raised us as Catholics too."

"Wait a minute." Cam spread his hands on the table. "You're *strega*?"

"Well, yeah," Ursula said, her eyebrows raised as she shrugged. "Nonna taught us everything she knew when she realized we had magic too."

"We?" Cam asked.

"Me and my sister," Ursula answered, innocently revealing way too much to this stranger.

John cursed under his breath. If the fey was playing a

game with them, he'd just learned there were not one but two powerful witches in town. John hoped that knowledge wouldn't come back to bite them.

"How about we talk about the leviathan?" John broke in before any more personal information about the Ricoletti sisters could be given.

"Aye," Cam agreed somewhat reluctantly. "But 'tis good fortune you have *strega* here to combat it. Now I understand where all the power is coming from. Some of those Italian ladies have very unique powers. I take it one of yours is to throw permanent wards."

Ursula nodded to the implied question.

"Thank the Mother of All for that," Cam said, aiming his words skyward. "I'll admit, when I felt the disturbance in the magic up here yesterday, I was concerned. After this afternoon's session, I grew even more so. The powers you're throwing here are mighty and have drawn attention from all those who are sensitive to such things—both good and evil. I'm very much afraid that if you continue this work, you'll be dealing with some of those on the other side of this war in the not-too-distant future. I'd bet they're already on their way here, to investigate. Many *Venifucus* seek to steal power. You and your sister would make nice, juicy targets for an unscrupulous mage."

John didn't like the sound of that.

CHAPTER ELEVEN

"What exactly are the *Venifucus* now? I mean, I've heard scary stories all my life, and there are new reports from the Lords, but what's truth and what's fiction? What are they now? The bogeymen from my childhood tales, or some kind of paramilitary magical organization?"

Tom asked the questions, giving John a few minutes to try to calm his bear. Right now, the creature was roaring in defiance of anyone who would even think to target Ursula. For crying out loud, wasn't she in enough danger already?

"When the Destroyer first walked in this realm, she drew around her a band of supporters. Mages, a few other fey, werecreatures who walked the dark paths, even a few vampires and many misguided humans. Any who sought power without really caring where it came from. Those who liked bloodshed and killing. Evil beings. They formed the *Venifucus*—a secret society that quietly supported and aided the Destroyer as she came to power. Once she was on her rampage, they came out into the open somewhat, fighting the forces of Light directly wherever they could." Cam's words held everyone's attention. "The human organization called the *Altor Custodis* was formed around the same time to keep an eye on the magical beings. They had a policy of non-involvement, but they have been watching us for centuries, keeping track of our whereabouts and our family lines. Recently, some of yours discovered that the *Venifucus* have infiltrated the *Altor Custodis* at the highest levels and have been using their observations to target and eliminate anyone they thought might oppose them."

"We'd had reports from the Lords," Brody confirmed.

John hadn't wanted to believe it and hoped the conflict would stay far away from his little town. He'd spent most of his life fighting, as had most of his men. He'd wanted to retire, set up the town, find a mate, and spend the rest of his life raising cubs and just living happily ever after.

It seemed like that wasn't going to happen. Though he hadn't invited it, evil had found him and he couldn't do anything but oppose it. Fight it and defeat it. So they could all live in peace. Eventually.

"You bears have concentrated a lot of magical energy here in your cove," Cam went on quietly. "I'm not surprised the creature was attracted to it. I don't think I've ever come across a concentration of shifter magic quite this potent anywhere in the world...except maybe for the snowcat stronghold, but they're protected by their terrain. Few outsiders venture into the Himalayas, and nobody can get near their cliff-top village without being seen long before. You don't have that advantage here. You're wide open."

"So you think concentrating so many bear shifters here together is what did it?" Tom asked.

"Och, now. You know how magical you folk are. And you're usually more solitary. Even bears who live in small family groups have been targeted by the *Venifucus*. You should have a talk with Rocco Garibaldi about his kinsmen and how they were kidnapped a while back. That was a family of just three bear shifters, one only a teenager, who managed to escape. Even so, working with just the magic of the mother and father—being siphoned off through torture and evil magic—the *Venifucus* were trying to open a portal into the farthest realm. Imagine what they could do with the number of bear shifters you have gathered here. It's too tasty a treat for them not to try. You should warn your people."

"We're not civilians," Brody ground out, clearly angered by the idea that someone would harm innocents like Cam was describing. "We can take care of ourselves."

Cam nodded once. "Aye, but you've got non-soldiers in your town too, I'm sure. Like the lass, here." Cam turned his attention back to Ursula, his gaze speculative. "But I'm thinking the wards she's putting up will go a long way toward keeping you all safe within the boundaries. What have you been putting into your wards, lass?"

"Protection against evil, safety for all beings of good intent, that sort of thing," Ursula replied. "I kept it general because it's not just one kind of bear shifter here, and I don't know what might be out in the water besides the leviathan and its minions. There could be selkies or water sprites, or who-knows-what out there, just trying to live life in peace. I didn't want my wards to keep them away if they were good."

"You have a big heart, lassie," Cam said, smiling kindly at her. "That was well done of you, and I think it will aid more in the protection of this town than you think. If I'm right, there will be a natural barrier when you're done with your spellwork, that will help hide your town from those of evil intent. That would be the best outcome, in fact, and would go a long way in protecting the people here."

John hadn't realized the scope of Ursula's work, or that wards could have different intentions, though he supposed he probably should have thought of that before. He was just glad to hear that Ursula had given this whole thing some thought and come up with what sounded like the most reasonable approach. He liked that she thought enough of the town and its people—and whatever innocent life might live in the ocean around them—to have planned her work so carefully.

"Now," Cam said, drawing John's attention, "if I'm guessing your pattern correctly, you'll be planning a sunset ceremony for tomorrow, no?"

John didn't like the idea that this strange fey could predict their actions so easily, but it did make sense. And if Cam could figure it out, so could the leviathan—and anyone else looking to prevent Ursula from completing her work. *Damn.*

Ursula nodded in answer to Cam's question, her eyes wide. Clearly, the same thought had just occurred to her as well.

"We'll need to establish trust fairly quickly. Alpha, would you object if I transported some of your allies here tomorrow, with me, to help your men stand guard while we do our work? If you'll call Grif Redstone and ask if he can send Steve and maybe a few members of his security team, I'll be able to bring a couple of people with me tomorrow when I come back. I'm also hoping you'll take their word for my truthfulness. They'll vouch for me."

John was skeptical, but moving toward trusting the fey with each new revelation. Though he hadn't mentioned it, John and all his guys knew Steve Redstone fairly well from the old days. Steve and his brother, Grif, who was Alpha of the entire Redstone Clan, had both been in Special Forces. John had fought alongside Steve Redstone a few times during his long military career and respected the man, even if he was a cougar shifter and not a bear.

"Sounds like you're planning on leaving us?" John asked Cam, wanting to know more before he committed to the fey's plan.

"Well, I came to help the lassie, but as you've got all well in hand for tonight, there are a few things I need to do back in California this evening. But if you're going to do more warding tomorrow, I'll come back to help, and bring friends, if you'll have them. It's up to you, Alpha. This is your land, and these are your people."

John chuckled. "They may call me Alpha, but it's not like it is with the cats. Bears are independent thinkers. Only my military unit really listens to what I have to say, and even then, we discuss battle plans in depth. There are no blind followers among us. There never were." John turned to Brody and Tom. "What do you think, boys?"

"Steve Redstone is a good guy," Brody offered. "If he's

willing to come help, I wouldn't be averse to having him as backup."

"Agreed," Tom put in. "I'd also take his word if he vouched for you, Cam, no insult intended."

Cam nodded at Tom. "None taken."

"I think it's all overkill," Ursula said. "But we can use all the help we can get. If this guy Steve can convince you that Cam is on the level, then I say go for it, even though you didn't ask my opinion." She stuck her tongue out playfully at John, and he felt the jolt of happiness at the way she interacted with him and his men. She was comfortable with them, which meant a lot to him and his inner bear.

"Honey, I was going to ask you. You just didn't give me a chance," he shot back, smiling at her.

"Good," she answered back. "Then I'll have to tell you that I would like Cam's help tomorrow. The leviathan lured me in this afternoon when I thought I was safe from it. As magical as you guys are, you're not mages. I need magical help, and I can't imagine anything or anyone more magical than a fey knight." She smiled at Cam, and John felt the stirrings of jealousy. "And if it hasn't already occurred to you, he would never have gotten past the wards I've already cast if he was one of the bad guys. You probably don't realize how my magic works yet, but you'll figure it out when you see how the wards repel evil." She looked a tiny bit smug. "That's why the leviathan tried to lure me out, past the effective range of the ward. It wanted to get me into an unprotected area."

John put his arm around her shoulders, offering support as her expression changed to one of fear.

"You were stronger than its pull, honey. You stopped walking all on your own," he reminded her.

"But I couldn't move," she whispered. "And I might not have been able to hold out against it for long. You didn't hear that song..."

"It sang to you?" Cam asked quickly, in a low, urgent tone.

Ursula nodded. "Like a siren's song. It made me follow it through the woods, around the cove, where nobody would see me until it was too late."

Cam frowned. "Not good. If you could hear the leviathan, it is more powerful than I thought. Did any of you hear it?" He looked at the men, each in turn, but they all shook their heads.

"I found her, but I didn't hear anything," John admitted. "She was just standing there, motionless."

Cam seemed unhappy with the answer but said no more on the topic. After a moment, he spoke again. "Your granny, she's in Italy?" he asked Ursula.

"Oh, no. She's in San Francisco." John might've wanted to keep such information private, but Ursula apparently had no such intention. She trusted Cam. John just hoped she wouldn't come to regret it.

"San Francisco?" Cam sat back in his chair. "But…you're not a Ricoletti, by chance, are you?"

Ursula smiled. "I am." John could hear the pride in her tone as she claimed the relation.

Cam's reaction was unexpected. He practically beamed with happiness. "Oh, this is grand," he said. "I know your granny. Knew her when she was your age, in fact. I haven't kept in touch over the years, but that's mostly because I don't always like reminding my friends of their mortality. They usually don't take it well. I pass in and out of people's lives, for the most part, but I remember your granny." Cam winked at her as if sharing a joke…or a memory. "She was special."

"She still is," Ursula agreed in a quiet voice, giving Cam a kind smile. "And I think she would be happy to see you again, if you don't mind the fact that she's grown old."

"Mind?" Cam seemed surprised by the notion. "It is the way of things in this realm, lass."

That put a damper on the mood for a moment until Cam brightened a bit. "Now, let me tell you something few know, my new shifter friends." He looked around at John, Brody and Tom. "I can travel by magical means, but not easily and not often. Your realm limits me a trifle. I was able to pop up here because of the lass's prayer for help, and I will return on the same ticket, so to speak." Cam gave them a somewhat mysterious look. "I will be able to transport two or three others with me tomorrow, but there is no guarantee they'll be able to go back home that way. They'll probably have to go back the non-magical way. Which means, you'll have to put us up for the night tomorrow night, so we can be here both to help with the sundown ceremony tomorrow and for the full moon the following night. After that, we can make our way home by whatever means come to hand."

"Even you?" Tom asked quietly, seeming intrigued by the fey's open talk of magical transport.

This was something out of a storybook. As far as John knew, that kind of thing was limited only to the most powerful of mages and the truly magical races like the fey. But the fey weren't of this realm. They traveled here at their own peril and weren't able to access all of the magic they could command in their own world. John didn't know all there was to know about fey, but he knew that much.

"Aye, lad. Even me. This is your realm, not mine. I pay a price to walk among you, and hoofing it, or taking the bus, happens more often than you'd think." Cam had the grace to look embarrassed, but John figured the humble act was just that—an act. Still, it was nice of the fey to make the effort of letting them think he couldn't wipe the floor with them all magically, with one hand tied behind his back.

"I've got a place in town where you can stay," Zak volunteered. "I'm building a restaurant. It's not quite finished yet, but the upstairs apartment is good enough for guests, even though the furnishings are bare minimum. There's heat and running water. Beds in the bedrooms and a big couch in the living room. No cable TV yet though, sorry."

"If all goes as I expect, there won't be much time to be watching telly," Cam said with a laugh. "Thank you for the gracious offer. I accept."

John nodded over at Zak. It was a good solution. Zak could keep an eye on the visitors, and they'd be in the center of town, well within the already warded zone.

"Now I suggest you get on the phone and figure out who I should be picking up for the journey tomorrow," Cam said, rising from his seat. "I'm heading to Las Vegas, home base of the Redstone Clan. I'll be back on the morrow with as many as I can bring with me. I expect you to settle just who that is between yourselves and the Redstones. Sound good?"

John rose as well. "I can live with that." He liked that Cam wasn't forcing anyone on them.

"Then I'll take my leave of you until the morrow." Cam leaned across, offering his hand to John first, then to the other men as everyone rose. They all shook hands with new respect for each other. Cam simply nodded at Ursula, tipping an imaginary hat in her direction. "I'm glad you asked for help, and did not need much of it today. The Lady sent me here, I believe, because of what you will do tomorrow. She knows, lassie. She knows all and gives aid where it's needed. What you're doing here is bigger than you realize. And quite frankly, none of us expected the leviathan to be on our shores. I'll do some research tonight, but I believe, now that I think back, there was some talk of a creature like it in the Atlantic several months ago. I'll track that down," Cam said, looking at John. "We'll need all the information we can get about this menace."

"Agreed," John replied. "I'll place some calls myself. I had no idea anyone else had been dealing with this kind of thing."

"The oceans are vast, and most of us are land-based. It would probably be a good idea to try to speak with some of the ocean-going shifters, if at all possible. They probably know more about this than we do," Cam suggested.

John nodded.

"Thank you for coming to help," Ursula said in an emotional tone.

"It is my honor, lass," Cam said in all seriousness, nodding to her in an old world way. He held her gaze for a beat, then turned to the men, nodding at each in turn. "Until tomorrow."

Cam walked away, down the steps of the deck, toward the

forest. They all watched him go. As he entered the tree line, he seemed to glow, and for a split second, John saw the magical armor of a golden knight walking away from them, into the misty forest. Between one blink and the next, the knight was gone…and so was Cam.

"Did you just see…?" Tom trailed off in confusion, shaking his head.

"Dude in a full metal jacket, disappearing into the trees?" Zak replied, also shaking his head. "He sparkled like nobody's business. I've never seen anything like it."

"That was armor," Ursula supplied. "He's a Knight of the Light."

"No shit? Seriously?" was Tom's candid reply.

"What do you know about them?" John asked his friend, knowing Tom had always been the most studious of his buddies.

"*Chevalier de la Lumiere* is a sacred title earned by only a few souls in the mortal realm and beyond. It is an ancient order. Knights are chosen by the Lady Herself, it's said. Usually though, they hide their nature. I'm kind of surprised—and a little worried—that he's shown himself to us this way. Frankly, it also makes me suspicious, though I have no idea how someone could fake what we just saw."

"Anything evil couldn't get past my wards either," Ursula put in. "And you're right to worry. All *strega* know that when the Destroyer returns, the Knights will reveal themselves and work with those on the side of Light to fight Elspeth's evil again." Her brow furrowed as her words took on an ominous tone. "If the Knights are showing themselves, then perhaps the rumors out of Italy are true. Maybe Elspeth, Destroyer of Worlds, is back."

CHAPTER TWELVE

The first thing Urse did when she went inside was to grab her cell phone. She spared a moment to text Mel that she was okay and promised to call in a bit, but she had to talk to her grandmother first. Urse knew John and his friends were making a lot of phone calls too. They were interfacing with those Redstone people about who was going to join Cam tomorrow, and somebody was reporting to the Lords of the *were*, but Urse was more interested in the magical side of things, and what her Nonna thought about the knight showing up.

And Cam said he'd known Nonna when she was younger. Urse wanted to know more about that too, but when Nonna refused to say much about her prior acquaintance with the fey warrior, other than the fact that she had known him in her youth, Urse was disappointed. No matter how much she wiggled around the subject, Nonna would say no more.

She did, however, tell Urse to listen carefully to any suggestions Cam might make. She spoke very highly of his magical abilities and seemed both worried and glad that the fey knight had come to Urse's aid.

Nonna had also taken time to go over every step of the ceremony Urse would perform the next evening. She helped Urse rehearse the wording of her spell and discussed potential countermeasures that might be required, if the leviathan fought back directly as it had the first day.

Urse also described the spell song it had used on her that afternoon. Nonna was very interested in how Urse had been able to break away enough to stop walking toward the water. Nonna seemed impressed that Urse had been able to do so, even if she'd been frozen in place for a time. And Nonna was even more interested in the way John's shift had cut the magical cord that had been pulling her toward the leviathan.

After she finished the long call with Nonna, Urse called her sister and filled her in on everything that had happened. The first thing she did was release the ward on the doors to the bookstore so Mellie could get out if she wanted to leave. She hadn't meant to imprison her sister all afternoon. She'd have to come up with a better solution from now on. It wasn't fair to Mellie to be trapped like that, and Urse both begged for forgiveness and promised not to do it again.

Then came the question of when she was coming home. Urse squirmed for a bit, not sure how Mellie was going to take the news of her new relationship with John.

"Uh…would you mind if I stayed here at John's tonight? I could ask him to have some of his guys check on you if you don't want to be all alone there."

"Wait a minute," Mellie said. Urse could hear her sister's excited amusement through the phone line. "Do you mean to tell me that you and the mayor are getting it on?"

"Well…"

"Holy shit!" Mellie nearly shouted into the phone. Urse cringed and held the earpiece away from her head. "I can't believe it!" Mellie went on, gushing for a moment, then her voice dropped. "Does he growl when he comes?"

"Amelia!" Shocked, Urse used her sister's full name, scolding even as she blushed.

"Come on, you can tell me," Mellie wheedled, but no way was Urse discussing this. Not now. It was still too new.

"So that settles it then." Urse ignored Mellie's question. "I'll see you tomorrow morning. But I'll need a change of clothes…" She trailed off, thinking about logistics.

"I can pack a bag for you and have one of the guys bring it over. They seem to have set up a watch on the street. Every few minutes, one of the men strolls past, and it's not exactly casual."

"They're watching the store?" Urse grew alarmed.

"Oh, no. They're looking at the cove, mostly. Patrolling up and down the street, not just in front of the bookstore." That made Urse feel a little better. "I'll ask Peter the next time he drifts by, if he can run your things up to John's. I'm pretty sure he won't mind."

"You've got that Russian bear wrapped around your little finger already, don't you?" Urse chuckled.

"Don't I wish." Mel sighed playfully.

"Be good and stay indoors," Urse reminded her sister. "That thing in the cove almost lured me in earlier today. It has magic that can reach right through my wards. If it could get to me, it can probably get to you too, so promise me you'll be careful. In fact, why don't you see if you can go sleep over at the bakery again? It's not really safe to be alone."

"I'll do that," Mellie agreed. "But you're no fun. I want to hear all about you and the sexy mayor when you get back here tomorrow. I expect a full report."

Urse blew a raspberry into the phone before hanging up. Mellie knew Urse loved her, but no way was Urse going to entertain her sister's prurient curiosity about what John was like in the sack. Not now. Probably not ever.

She must have dozed off because the next thing Urse knew, she was being carried down the hallway in John's arms. She roused when he paused to open a door and looked around. He'd brought her to a bedroom. It was huge, as was the bed, and from the few belongings scattered around the neat room, she realized it must be John's.

He laid her on the bed and sat down beside her. His fingers traced gently over her face as he gazed into her eyes.

"How are you feeling?"

"Better." She reached up to hold his hand against her cheek. "Thank you for taking such good care of me."

"Thank *you* for taking such good care of my town. I had no idea when we started this that it would take so much out of you. Are you sure you can do the next two ceremonies in such short order?" His eyes narrowed, and a frown wrinkled his brow.

She sat up in the bed, facing him. "I recover quickly. It's just the immediate power drain that's so hard on me." She tried her best to reassure him, but he was still frowning. "Besides, I really have no other choice. The moon will be full night after tomorrow, and every day I wait is a day the cove is still in danger from the monster."

John moved closer. "You do have a choice, honey. You could always walk away and leave us to deal with this on our own."

Was he testing her? She thought he knew her better than that by now.

"No, I couldn't." Her tone was hard, but he was smiling now.

"I figured that's what you'd say." He placed one big hand at the back of her head and drew her in for a quick, hot kiss. "You're fierce, babe. I love that about you."

Her breath caught at his use of the L word, but he didn't give her time to think about it. He lowered his head and kissed the living daylights out of her.

And before too long, all thought was banished. Only sensations were left. The feel of his body pressing down over hers. The sudden discovery that he had done away with both of their clothes while he'd been kissing her. The slide of his rough skin over her smoother bits. The sensual delight as he gently claimed her body with his, coming into her in a slow, steady wave.

Like the water lapping at the shore, he began a rhythm that gradually increased, making her moan as he made love to her. And it really did feel like love. There was something different about this night as compared to last. Something familiar, yet incredibly unique. Some melding of energies that turned the building passion into an inferno of desire.

Before all coherent thought fled, she registered the differences and did her best to try to keep up with the raging ecstasy that wanted to break free.

And then, it did.

With a cry of his name, she came, realizing he followed her into bliss only a few seconds later. They were together in all things now, including the ultimate fulfillment. He held her throughout, keeping them joined as the passion peaked, then dropped, then peaked again.

She fell asleep again, his body still joined to hers, and that was the last thing she knew until morning.

John lay awake for a long time, running his finger lightly over the soft skin of her arm, wondering where this relationship was going. She was his mate. He didn't doubt that now. But how could a powerful witch mate with an Alpha bear? John was torn between the responsibility he felt toward his men, the town they had all built together, and the deep-seated yearning for his mate.

There was one factor in her favor though. He'd spent a few minutes looking up information about her ancestors. The bear shifter, in particular. Francisco. Turned out he was quite the hero back in the day. Francisco and his mate, Violetta, were both mentioned with great respect in the history of their people.

Francisco and Violetta had worked together—shifter and mage—to keep their people safe. John wanted that with Ursula. Oh, he didn't want to be famous or mentioned in the histories. He just wanted to live a happy, fulfilled life, full of joy and laughter, with his mate. He wanted her to be by his side, his helpmate, as he would be to her.

He feared they were living in *interesting times*, as the ancient curse went. Evil was stirring and targeting his people. He would do all he could to defend this place and the people who had made it their home. He liked that Ursula was prepared to do the same. He liked the way they'd worked together today and yesterday. He liked that she'd been able to draw on his innate magical energy and use it to craft something that would protect the cove for years to come.

He just plain liked everything about her. But the question remained in his mind... Could they make this work like her ancestors of old had? Could a bear shifter and a *strega* really be mates in this modern age?

He sincerely hoped so.

*

As they sat eating breakfast, looking out at the view of the cove the next morning, John filled Urse in on the people they were expecting to arrive that day. He seemed almost excited to welcome them, and Urse could hear the pride in his voice as he talked about showing them around town. Particularly the one he called Red.

"Red is Steve Redstone," John told her. "He's the second in command and second oldest of the Redstone brothers. Both he and his older brother, Grif, served in Special Forces, but Grif retired before Steve. They're cougar shifters, but their Clan encompasses all sorts of Packs, Clans and Tribes. You've heard of Redstone Construction, right?"

She nodded. "They're like one of the biggest construction firms in the country."

"That's the one. The brothers run it. Five werecats with majorly Alpha tendencies, and somehow, they make it work." John sounded like he admired the set up. "Cats aren't that dissimilar to us. They like to roam alone from time to time, just like bears."

Urse was interested in all the information John was sharing. Something had definitely changed overnight. He'd been forthcoming with her before, but now, he was letting her in on the inner workings of his mind and telling her things about his people that he probably wouldn't have told her just a day or two ago. She liked it. She felt like he trusted her, and she really, *really* liked that.

It was a sign of a strengthening of their relationship. It was a sign of commitment. A sign that she meant more to him than just a momentary fling.

"So seeing what they'd accomplished gave you inspiration for what you're doing here?" she asked, curious.

"In a way. If a bunch of Alpha cats can subdue their dominance in favor of working with their family, I figured me and my guys—who are just like family to me—could do it too. Bears are better than cats, right?" He grinned in a way that told her he was definitely teasing.

"I bet that's exactly the sales pitch you used." She shot him a grin.

"Guilty as charged." He smiled as he went back to eating the mountain of scrambled eggs and bacon he'd made.

Urse had taken about a quarter of the plate he'd originally set before her and shoveled the rest onto his plate. He'd frowned a bit until she told him there was no way in hell she'd ever eat that much in one sitting. From all appearances, he had no problem eating her portion in addition to the giant one he'd served himself.

"So who else is coming?" she asked, curious about the other new shifters who would be coming to town with Cam.

The very idea that Cam could transport both himself and others magically still boggled her mind, but this was her first encounter with a real live fey. Who knew, really, how deep their magic ran? She'd heard all sorts of fantastical stories about fey since she was a child, but she wasn't sure what was real and what was just exaggeration.

"An owl shifter named Joe Nightwing," John surprised her by saying. "I don't know him personally, but I've heard good things about him."

"I didn't know there was such a thing as an owl shifter," she admitted.

"They're a great help with aerial recon," was John's rather prosaic comment. "The third guy is a fellow I know by reputation. He's a mercenary. He leads a group that's a mixed bag of various kinds of shifters. His name is Seth, and they call him The Golden Jackal."

"Is that some kind of code name?" Urse asked, intrigued by the mysterious moniker.

John snorted. "Yeah, but it's also what he is—his beast half is a golden jackal. He's Turkish, I think. I always thought it was kind of stupid to advertise what he was like that, but they say Seth has a rather ironic sense of humor. It'd be like me calling my group Papa Bear and the Grizzlies." He snorted again, laughing into his coffee mug.

"Sounds like a 50's doo wop group," she joked, chuckling with him.

"I was surprised he was here in the States, actually. Seth is one of those guys who operates in the Middle East most of the time. He speaks a bunch of languages and can infiltrate where we Westerners can't always go. Seems he's been in the States for a while now and had traveled to Las Vegas to share intel with the Redstones. He was heading to Wyoming next, but he was willing to stop off here first and help with our little problem." John finished off the last of his coffee. "He's probably interested in gathering intel here too. The Jackal's specialty is recon, so I'm not surprised he's in the middle of this—whatever this turns out to be. I suspect if the Destroyer is really back in this realm, he'd be the first to know for sure and have proof."

"When do you expect them to arrive?" The question was no sooner out of her mouth than she felt a big fanfare of magic flaring, as if the sounding of magical trumpets. "Never mind," she said, shaking her head. "They're here."

John's phone rang before he could even ask her how she knew. He picked it up, giving her a raised eyebrow look.

Urse went into action, clearing the empty breakfast dishes and loading the dishwasher while John held a conversation with the sheriff. It looked like their busy day had just begun.

Cameron had poofed in at the town hall this time, along with his three companions. Brody had drawn his weapon on them when they just suddenly appeared, but recognizing Steve Redstone, he put up the muzzle almost immediately, swearing roundly. The guys were still having a good laugh about his reaction when John and Ursula walked into the town hall about ten minutes later.

John greeted them all, letting Steve Redstone do the formal introductions to the two new shifters. Brody had called Zak in, as well as the rest of their core group. The Spec Ops bears had always worked and traveled as a group, while guys like Seth went from team to team and place to place around the world until he'd gone out on his own, gathering a group of likeminded misfits around himself.

With the arrival of Steve and the other shifters, who seemed to know a lot more about Cam than John did, his bear instincts began to settle. Although he would wait and see how Cam behaved, the acceptance and recommendation of the other shifters went a long way toward making John feel better.

John ushered them all into the war room they'd set up at town hall, Ursula with them as the notable sole female. She didn't seem to mind, but John realized other women—bear women—wouldn't be so accepting of the lopsided way the military created its Spec Ops teams. John didn't have anything against women in combat. Bear females could be even more lethal and destructive than many males. But the human military didn't usually allow women in combat roles—especially not in Special Forces.

That was one of the reasons John had concocted this retirement strategy. In a village setting, he'd hoped to even out the numbers of males and females, with the aim of helping some of his guys find mates. A lot of them had been soldiering for way too long. Some of them had horrific experiences in their pasts that would probably only begin to be healed by the intervention of an understanding, loving female touch.

"Tonight's festivities will happen at sunset," Cam stated, drawing everyone's attention as they sat around the big conference table in the war room. "The third and final ceremony of the sun will be the culmination of the good work Lady Ursula has done so far. With our help, she may be able to direct the energies of her last two spells into a new protective barrier that will prevent anything like what happened yesterday to bring me here, from happening again."

"What exactly did you hear, Ursula?" John asked her softly, knowing they all needed to know as much as she could tell them so they could be on the lookout and not fall victim to what had almost happened to her.

"It was a song. Like I imagine a siren's song might sound, but wordless. More like an indistinct whispering. If the whispers were some kind of communication, they weren't in any language I've ever heard before. They might have been in some language from another realm."

"That is more likely than not," Cam confirmed, frowning. "Such language is not fit for mortal ears. Be glad you could not hear it clearly. Such a thing could confound you permanently, leaving you trapped in your own mind. Mad." He looked around the table, catching every eye. "My advice to you, should any of you suspect you are hearing the voice of the leviathan, hold your ears and do everything in your power not to listen, if possible."

"The pull was like nothing I've ever felt before. I started out following it, trying to figure out what it was, and suddenly, I found myself halfway around the cove, in the woods. It led me out of sight of everyone else, into the woods and around to where my ward no longer held the creature at bay. If the bond hadn't been broken by John's shifting in its path, I shudder to think what would have happened." Ursula shivered in her seat.

"'Tis to your credit you were able to wake yourself from the leviathan's song before you were out of the woods," Cam commented.

"It felt like something was wrong, but at first, I couldn't figure out what it was. Eventually, I woke up and I stopped walking, doing everything I could to resist, but I was frozen. I couldn't move until John found me and shifted, breaking the spell," she admitted, smiling softly at John, like he was some kind of hero or something.

John felt that smile all the way down to his bones. That his mate would look at him like that was...well...it was an amazing feeling. It was something he wanted to see for the rest of his life. He wanted to be worthy of that kind of look from her all the time. He would do everything in his power to be her real life hero from now until eternity.

Cam cleared his throat, gently bringing John back to the conference room and the meeting that was in progress. Only Ursula had that effect on him. Only his mate could distract him from a room full of shifters holding a war plan session.

John shook his head, amused at himself. He couldn't get upset about it. Finding his mate was a momentous thing. It might be a little inconvenient to be so distracted during a crisis like this, but he couldn't feel bad about it. He'd found his mate! He'd cut himself a little slack on everything else—as long as he was still able to keep everyone safe.

They kept making plans and accounting for all sorts of contingencies that might never come to pass. Joe Nightwing was going to do aerial recon, as John had expected. He would be reporting to Brody, who was going to coordinate the ground troops while John was once again in the center of the circle with Ursula.

The Jackal was surprisingly easy to work with. He was smooth-tongued and had a wickedly sharp wit and eye for strategy that John came to quickly respect. He, too, would be reporting to Brody, but he was going to be paired with Zak, running recon. Having the two newcomers on recon would free up John's men for defense.

"I'd like to split up our forces into two groups. Alpha team will be led by Brody. Red, if you're up for it, I'd like you to lead Beta." John nodded toward Steve Redstone, using the nickname he'd gone by in the military.

"It'd be an honor," Red answered right away, as John had known he would.

Red might be a cat, but he was a born leader of men. He didn't do well in the background. He had to be one of the guys leading the charge. It was where his true talent lay, and John was happy to exploit the strengths of every single one of the men under his command.

Not that they were still in the military, but this was sure starting to feel like one of their old ops. They hadn't gone up against magic often, but occasionally, there were unseen forces their unit had to deal with when regular human troops were getting their asses handed to them. Most of the brass never knew why John's team was so damn good at the impossible missions. They just knew he got results.

There was one officer though...a Navy admiral...who knew the score. He was in the command structure, and he knew exactly who to call when magic came into play. He was the one John had called when the leviathan had first appeared, but though he was willing to send his best people, they were otherwise engaged in real world activities at the moment and wouldn't be free to come out to Grizzly Cove anytime soon. Those were the guys they needed. John could feel it in his bones.

Until those guys were available, the residents of Grizzly Cove simply had to do what they could to protect themselves from the creature. Ursula was putting herself and her magic on the line to do just that, and he couldn't be more proud of her. She was one hell of a woman.

"Now..." Cam said, breaking into John's thoughts. "I believe you have a sample of one of the smaller creatures on ice somewhere. Is it possible we could take a wee look? See what we're up against?"

"Sure." John signaled to Brody, who was closest to the door. Brody got up and left the room. "We sent about half of it up to the Lords after Zak here managed to rip one of the tentacles off the smaller creature that had attacked his mate, but nobody in Montana had never seen anything like it, and the High Priestess is away at the moment. We're hoping to get more information once she has a chance to look at it."

At that point, Brody returned, carrying a heavy duty trash bag in his hands. He placed it on the table in front of Cam, pulling it open to show what was inside.

Cam scrambled from his chair, standing up in what appeared to be alarm. John watched, seeing the fey's face pale.

"Uh, Brody, you want to move that a little farther away from him?" John said into the stunned silence. Nobody had expected the cool, collected fey to nearly jump out of his skin like that.

"Sorry," Brody mumbled, taking the bag back and moving it down the table a good five feet. Cam watched it with an intense expression.

"Dear Mother in heaven," the fey muttered as the tentacle fragment moved farther away. "I never thought to see such things in this realm again."

"What is it?" Steve asked, looking into the trash bag that was now closer to him.

"I thought..." He trailed off and started over. "I'd hoped you were exaggerating. Or just plain wrong, but this... This is definitely from one of the leviathan's minions. Something from another realm. An evil thing from a place of evil. A creature of chaos and hunger that never ends." Cam was staring at the bag, his face still pale. "Such things should not be here in the mortal realm. This is very bad indeed. It means the Destroyer's followers are even stronger than we suspected. Otherwise, they could not have summoned such a demon."

"Any tips on how to send it back where it came from?" John asked. "The *strega* seem to think it cannot be killed, only banished."

"Oh, aye. That's the way of it. Its power is connected to its own realm and, as such, cannot be severed from here. It needs to be sent elsewhere, but it is not a job for just anyone. That would require a very special skill set and balls the size of Kentucky."

John couldn't help but laugh at the unexpected comment,

and finally, the tension broke. Cam seemed to calm, and a bit of his normal color returned, though he remained on his feet until John gave Brody the nod, and he took the bag back to the empty fridge, where it had been stored.

"Trisha should probably take a look at this," Steve offered. "My mate is Admiral Morrow's daughter. She has powers over water, like her brothers." Then Steve frowned. "But I don't want her in danger."

"I called Admiral Morrow when this all started," John told him, nodding. "The Admiral promised to send one of his sons here as soon as they were done with their current assignment, but they're out of communication for a while yet. Deep undercover."

"Probably deep underwater," Steve commented with a chuckle.

"That was the impression I got," John agreed. "They're coming, but I don't know when."

"Well, then, if you've got a Navy SEAL water sprite on the way, we'll just leave the creature to him," Cam declared. "Either one of them has the skill set I was talking about, no doubt. If anyone can rid this world of the leviathan once again, it will be one—or maybe both—of Trisha's brothers. I've met the lady, and her power is formidable." Cam nodded respectfully to Steve.

"We just have to do what we can until then," John put in.

"Aye," Cam agreed with him, nodding again. "And the lassie's wards will go a long way toward safeguarding this cove for generations to come. What we're doing here right now is not trivial. In fact, it is vital if you wish to keep this town going. Concentrating this much magical power in one place will require ongoing protection."

"I guess I didn't really think of that when I came up with this idea." John felt a little sheepish for having overlooked such a big thing.

He knew intimately how magical bears were. He should've thought about how grouping them together in one spot might attract the wrong sort of attention. But in his defense, the plans for the town had been in place for a very long time—years longer than anyone even thought there might be a threat from something like the *Venifucus*.

"Don't feel bad, Alpha," Cam absolved him. "Under normal circumstances, you and your people probably could have handled whatever came your way. None of you could have foreseen some damn fool would be mad enough to release the leviathan."

CHAPTER THIRTEEN

When lunch was brought in for the guys, Urse decided to leave. John insisted on walking her back to the bookstore, where she could rest up for the evening's work. He dropped her off at the door, insisting she enter before he would leave and making Amelia promise to keep her sister there and call him if Urse stepped even one toe outside the store.

The kiss he gave her before leaving set her toes on fire and left her feeling a little bit giddy, but any promise of passion fulfilled it made would have to wait until later.

Surprisingly, Mellie didn't give her any guff about her new relationship with John. Mellie just gave her a big hug and told her she'd already made lunch. Urse had to smile. Nonna had taught them well. The best comfort an Italian woman could offer her family was to feed them.

Mellie had gone all out on lunch. She'd prepared all of Urse's favorite dishes, knowing she wouldn't be able to eat again until after the sunset ceremony.

"Thanks, Mel." Urse almost sniffled when she saw the awesome lunch Mellie had prepared, but settled for hugging her sister again, briefly.

After she ate, Urse prepared the few things she'd need for the evening, repacked her overnight bag in case she ended up at John's again, and then did a little tidying up around the

155

apartment before she settled in for a nap. She needed to be rested before she attempted to lay another ward in the presence—and defiance—of the leviathan. She hadn't really told anyone how drained she felt after each session, but the effect was becoming greater. She just had to get through tonight and then the big full moon ceremony tomorrow...

She prayed to the Mother of All that she had the strength.

When Urse woke, John was there, sitting on the side of her bed, smiling softly, though she could read concern in his warm brown eyes.

"How are you feeling?" The warm growl of his voice swept over her senses like a velvet caress.

That new part of her that seemed to be growing stronger in his presence stretched to meet him. The tiny part of her soul that touched the bear spirit was happy whenever they were near John. Of course, John seemed to make every part of Urse happy. He was so safe and warm. He was also caring and so handsome she could still hardly believe he was real.

"Better," she told him. "I was just a little tired. What time is it?"

"About an hour 'til sunset. I left the guys to prepare and figured I'd come over and help you get ready, if you needed help."

"I already set up the few things I'll need. I just have to freshen up and get dressed, then we should probably get moving. I want to be up at the site in plenty of time."

John stood and moved back while she sat up and got out of bed. She paused long enough to step close to him and give him a hug. He seemed bemused by it, but he wrapped his strong arms around her and let her snuggle into his warmth for a moment.

"Thank you for coming to get me," she whispered, closing her eyes and resting her cheek against the steady beat of his heart. He was such a good man. So strong and yet so tender with her.

"Anytime, honey."

They stood for a few moments longer before she

reluctantly drew away to start getting ready. John went out into the living room to chat with Mellie while Urse did her thing.

After she'd put on the fresh clothing she'd laid out before falling asleep, she went out to find John. He escorted her to the door, and Mellie followed them down, giving Urse a hug.

"Be careful, sis," Mellie whispered.

"You too. Don't leave the building."

"I'm leaving Peter with you," John put in, directing his words to Mel. "I don't trust the leviathan as far as I could throw it. Until we're sure it can't reach either of you, someone will be watching over you at all times."

Mel stood back and nodded at John. "Thanks."

Urse would have expected her sister to object, but Mellie was just as scared of the leviathan as she was now. That thing was dangerous and had proven it could reach through the wards with its song to lure Urse away. If it could do that, it could probably do the same to Mel. Better to have a bear shifter guard watching her, and Urse suspected Mel liked Peter even more than she was letting on.

They left without further comment and headed for John's SUV. He drove them around to the northern point of the cove, where tonight's work would be done. They didn't talk much on the way. Urse was going over what she had to do in her mind and trying to calm down. Her nerves were fried, which wasn't a good mindset with which to go into a major magical working.

"It's gonna be all right," John said, covering one of her hands with his as he pulled to a stop in the woods near the northern point of the cove. Other cars were already there, in a small clearing, meaning his guys were already in the area, securing the perimeter.

"How do you know?" She allowed a bit of her doubt to show. She felt safe enough with John to let him in.

"Because I'll be with you every step of the way. When we're together, there's nothing we can't accomplish. And we have allies." He nodded toward the tree line. "Cam's already here. I know we just met the guy, but I have a feeling he's going to come in handy."

His attitude helped a lot. "Thanks. I needed the reminder. This has already taken a lot out of me, and I was worried…"

"Honey, I know this is draining you. I'm sorry for it. Sorrier than I can say. But I don't think your Nonna, or the Mother of All, would set a task before you that you couldn't accomplish. You said your grandmother knew your magic better than anyone else, right? She was the one who laid out the initial plan. She's never given you reason to think she doubts your ability to see it through. If she has confidence in you, so should you."

Now *that* was something she hadn't thought of in quite that way.

"You know…you're right. Nonna wouldn't set me up for failure. And we decided on this course even before she knew Cam was here—or what you and your men truly could contribute. I think there's power enough to spare on our side. At least, I hope so."

He squeezed her hand. "I know so." His tone was full of the confidence she needed so much to hear. "It may tire you and stretch you to your limits, but you've got this, baby. And I'm right there with you. I won't fail you. Ever."

She reached across the center console and kissed him. He was such a good man.

"How did I get so lucky as to have you here, exactly when I need you?" She whispered her thoughts, but she knew he heard her. He kissed her back, taking just a moment to give her a proper, toe-curling kiss.

Urse felt the ripple of magic that told her Cam was nearby as she moved away from John. Sure enough, the fey knight was standing about ten feet from the SUV, in plain sight, pretending not to see what they'd been doing. The magical "knock" had been his polite way of letting her know he was there.

She sent Cam a smile and then opened the door and hopped down from the tall vehicle. John got out on the driver's side and came around to walk with her toward the trees.

"Is everything ready?" John asked the man standing behind Cam. It was a bear shifter she hadn't met before but knew from seeing him around town.

"All set to go," the man replied. He looked awfully familiar, and when Brody stepped out of the trees and came to stand next to him, she immediately saw the family resemblance.

They must've seen her eyes widen because Brody tipped his hat toward her. "Have you met my brother, Jack? He's the Game Warden."

"Nice to meet you, Jack. Thanks for helping with this," she told him, giving him a warm smile.

"Happy to be of service, ma'am." Jack tipped his hat much the way Brody had done.

When they arrived at the site, Urse realized the exposure in this particular setup. They were on a small triangular spit of rocky land that marked the northern side of the mouth of the cove. There were no trees nearby. The land dropped off abruptly to a narrow strip of beach that lay about five feet below the rocky ground she would be standing on.

The ocean was already churning, and she sensed the approach of the leviathan and its minions beneath the waves. She began to understand it had left the smaller creatures nearer to shore to keep watch while it went out into the ocean to do Goddess-only-knows-what. And now that the shifters, herself and Cam were present, the minions were calling to its master.

"We don't have a lot of time." She nearly had to shout to be heard above the crashing of the waves as it increased in intensity. "It knows we're here, and it's coming."

"Aye," Cam said, appearing at her side. "Cast your circle, milady. I'll protect from without as best I can while you and your bear work the magic within."

Urse wanted to question Cam's decision, but there was no time. She'd thought he'd be inside the circle with her, helping her, but instead, he was going to be outside? That was disappointing, to say the least. But he knew his own abilities better than she did. Maybe there was something he could do from outside the circle that would help more. She had no idea what that might be, but she had to trust that she—and John—would be enough to seal this side of the entrance to the cove with one of her most powerful wards and make it safe.

She'd been going through what she would do since last night. She cast a much smaller circle this time, making sure John was close to her. He said nothing for the moment. He just helped as he had before, in spreading the salt and standing by, offering his silent support.

"Get your guys as far away from the beach as you can," she told him as she cast. He was wearing a radio that would be useless once she closed the circle, but for now, he could still communicate with his men. She had to warn him that this time was different. "The leviathan is coming. It's going to put up one hell of a fight and anyone outside this circle will be in very serious danger."

"What about Cam?" John asked, already fingering his radio.

She shrugged, turning to him in confusion, letting her fear show for just a moment. "I have no idea what he's capable of, but he said he's staying outside the circle. I can only assume he has defenses of his own, but everyone else will be super vulnerable. Keep them well back. They can't help when the magic starts flying anyway. Do it now, John. I'm nearly finished with the circle."

She started moving again, knowing he was talking fast and low over his radio. She looked up and received his nod before she lay the last grains of salt and said the final incantation.

She had no sooner closed the circle before the leviathan became visible in the distance. It was closing fast.

"Sweet Mother of All," she whispered, watching it approach, frozen for a moment. John stepped up behind her and wrapped his arms around her waist. He dipped his head close to her ear and spoke in low, urgent tones.

"Don't let it intimidate you, honey. Often the biggest shows are put on by the weakest opponents. This is all designed to scare you and make you falter. Don't let it get to you. It wouldn't try so hard to stop you if you weren't seriously cramping its style. Do your thing, babe. I'm right here, with you."

She stayed one moment longer in his arms, gathering courage from his presence and his words. He was so good to her. He knew just what to say to bolster her.

Patting his hands, she stepped forward toward the ocean, meeting the advance of the creature with purpose in her steps. She positioned herself at the center of the circle and began to chant.

The words were ancient. Powerful. She had thought out each in advance and done all she could to craft the perfect sequence of prayers, benedictions, beseeching and commanding of the power that flowed through her by the will of the Goddess. She began to feel the power exerting itself through her, up into the center of the dome of protection she had spun, gathering strength and steam until it was ready to be unleashed.

As before, she felt John's support as his magic came out to play with hers. They were even more attuned to each other than before, and she was able to take more of his raw energy and fashion it into what would become one of the strongest wards she had ever produced—if she could follow through and cast the spell before the leviathan did something to thwart her.

She felt the creature's assault on her circle of protection. It battered at her, to no avail. She worried briefly for the men who were outside the circle, but she hoped they were all smart enough to know when to stand back.

All except Cam. She felt his presence behind her circle, moving swiftly around as the leviathan grew closer. What was he up to?

He came around the side of her circle closest to the sea,

and she understood. He was the ace in the hole. The surprise to distract and enrage the creature. While Cam did battle with it on a magical level, she would have to act to protect the cove. Timing would be everything.

The creature seemed to stop in its tracks the moment Cam was revealed. And then, all hell broke loose once more. The creature seemed to jump up out of the water, trying to reach the fey warrior on the land.

It was hideous. All she could see were myriad tentacles and razor sharp projections. It couldn't come completely out of the ocean, so all she saw were the parts it could project upwards and outwards, but that was more than enough. She'd be having nightmares about it for the rest of her life, she was sure.

She spent a moment worrying about Cam, but then, she realized the fey was more than equipped to serve as a diversion while she did her thing. She'd better get on with it, or all his daring would be for naught.

Urse concentrated on her spellcraft, drawing on the energy of the earth, the sky, the wind and even the water. She called upon the willing gift of magical energy from the Alpha and, through him, from his people. She didn't take too much from them. They needed to be able to defend themselves, and there was still tomorrow to consider, when they would be called upon again to donate power to the protection of their town.

She took what she judged to be enough. She had a specific goal in mind for tonight. A geographical area she wished to protect with her spell that covered exactly half of the mouth of the cove. The other half would be done tomorrow—and then some. Tomorrow night, when she had the power of the full moon to call upon, and no spellwork to do the following day, she would create the biggest overlap she could to be certain the cove had as much protection as she could provide.

For tonight, she knew exactly how far to push herself and her helpers. She spoke the words, her confidence increasing as she felt the way John's power merged so much more seamlessly with hers. It was beautiful, really, but she didn't have time to sit and study it. Perhaps that would come later. When the danger was past.

When she was ready, she loosed the spell, only peripherally aware of Cam's golden armor glowing just outside the circle as he faced the monster. Whether his armor manifested to everyone or if her ability to see it was a byproduct of the immense power she wielded, she didn't know, but she was glad to see that mark of the Goddess as she flung her spell in the very teeth of the leviathan.

It...screamed. Although that word didn't quite cover the intense cacophony of sound and evil that emanated from the creature as it fell back, hit by the power of her ward.

It crashed back into the ocean, water coming up in a mini tsunami, washing over the point of the cove on which they stood. Urse held strong, knowing her circle would keep her and John safe. She wasn't sure about the rest of the men. She prayed they were far enough back to avoid being washed into the cove or ocean by the powerful wave.

Cam was another story. He glowed with golden light as the water parted around him. Encased in her bubble of protection, she could see Cam clearly. He was protected, too, though he had no circle. Perhaps it was his armor—blessed by the Mother of All—that was his shield. She would probably never know.

"Isn't that something?" John whispered as the water passed over their invisible, magical dome. He was looking at Cam and up at the water sliding over and off the shield to wet only the area outside the circle.

"Pretty cool, huh?" she agreed wearily. The magic was spent. The ward had been placed. The leviathan had been run off. For now.

"I take it we're done for the night?" John asked, coming up behind her again. He'd been a strong presence at her side throughout, but now, he put his arms around her, supporting her as she began to wilt.

"Yeah. The ward is up and running. We're safe here for

now. We just have to break the circle and make sure all your men are still with us. I'm afraid some of them might've gotten washed away by the wave."

John walked her over to the side of the circle closest to Cam. The fey was watching them with a grin on his face. His hands were on his hips, satisfaction in every line of his body.

Urse broke the circle with a final prayer of thanks, and the magic dome collapsed back into the earth. Cam was no longer glowing with power, but the expression on his face was one of approval.

"That was beautifully done, lassie. Beautifully done," Cam repeated, smiling from ear to ear.

Urse felt bolstered by the fey knight's words, but she was weary to the bone. If John hadn't been standing behind her, propping her up, she'd have slipped to the ground like a limp noodle.

Cam seemed to realize it belatedly and turned his attention to the ocean while John spoke into his radio, checking on his men. Urse rested against him, waiting to hear that all the shifters who'd come out to support them were okay.

"Everyone's accounted for," John said quietly near her ear. "Joe Nightwing is going to fly out and see how far the safe zone extends."

"I wouldn't advise it," Cam said, talking directly to John. "That thing can reach pretty high. It's not worth the risk."

"I'll call him back," John promised, speaking quickly into his radio in a sort of clipped code that he and his men seemed to understand. It must be a military thing, Urse thought.

A few seconds later, they saw an enormous owl glide silently overhead. He dipped one wing as if in acknowledgment before flying off, over the forest, toward the town.

"Shall we?" John asked politely before lifting her in his arms. She felt foolish, but too weak to really argue.

He walked back toward where they'd left the vehicle, Cam at their side. The men spoke in low tones while she dozed in John's arms. If he hadn't been there to carry her back, she probably would've slept out on the point tonight. She was way too weak after that spell to walk out through the forest on her own.

Thank the Goddess she only had to do one more of these. She didn't think she'd have the strength to do any more. But she was still a bit worried... Tomorrow night would be the biggest expenditure of magical energy of all.

*

"Wake up, baby. I know you're tired, but you really should eat something. We missed dinner."

John's voice came to her, rousing Urse out of the fog of sleep. She discovered she was in his house, lying on the couch in his living room. He'd put a blanket over her at some point, and she figured she'd been asleep for a few hours at least.

Delicious aromas hit her nose, and her stomach growled a little. Someone had cooked. She heard John talking in low tones with another man, and then, she heard the door open and close, and she felt, from the drop in ambient magic, that they were alone. Her magical senses were more sensitive than usual after all the wards she'd been casting these past few days.

She padded into the kitchen and found a gourmet feast had been laid out on the big butcher block table.

"I asked Zak to cook something special for you. The man's a genius in the kitchen."

"You did?" She looked from the food up to his beloved face. "He did all this for you? For us?" She felt tears gather in her eyes. She didn't know why she was so emotional, but it just seemed like such a big thing for Zak to do for John—and for John to arrange for her. "He must love you a lot to go to all this trouble after the day we've had."

John actually blushed, looking down and busying his hands by setting out plates and silverware. "I might've asked, but he did it for you. All my guys know how hard you're pushing yourself to safeguard our little town. This is Zak's way of saying thank you."

"Well, it's pretty spectacular—and very welcome at the moment. I'm starved." She moved closer, taking a seat at the table. "My goodness, is that Cajun rice? And beef stroganoff? Wow."

John served portions of whatever she asked for, placing it all on her plate before making his own serving. He sat beside her at the giant table, and they shared a lovely meal, quietly, together.

It was a cozy feeling, being here with him, in the home he had built. She could feel the love and hope that had gone into every timber, brick, cut and nail. This was a place of potential. Potential for joy and for the future. A dream come to fruition, needing only a few more key elements to make reality.

Much like the town John had dreamed. He'd shared his dream with his men, and they'd built it into something real. Something beautiful. All because he'd dared to dream it.

John was a man who made things come to pass. He wasn't a bystander in his own life—or in the lives of those he touched. The others had followed him into battle and now, into life as civilians precisely because of his ability to lead. To dream big and make things happen.

He was a hell of a man, and she greatly feared she was falling deeply in love with him. So deep, her love for him would change her for all time.

Uncomfortable with the direction of her thoughts, she broke the silence with idle conversation.

"So what happened to Cam? I almost expected him to be somewhere nearby, already planning the next event." She picked at her food as she continued to eat. It really was delicious. She'd have to thank Zak specially, for going out of his way.

"He probably is already planning, but he's staying in town tonight with the guys he brought in. Zak's christening the new kitchen he's almost finished building in the restaurant, entertaining everyone who's off duty. Sounds like they have a little party going on down there with Red in town."

"I can hear it in your voice, how much you like the guy. So you go way back?" She knew she was prodding him for information, but talking about the past was easier right now than thinking about the future.

John didn't seem to mind. "Red and his older brother, Grif, are good guys. Both found their mates since the last time any of us saw each other, so I think the guys are having a little party in honor of that momentous occasion, even though Red's mate is back in Las Vegas with the rest of the family." John spoke calmly, eating between sentences. His steady words calmed her as well, for which she was grateful. "I don't blame him for not wanting her here. What I've heard about her leads me to believe she'd be right out there in the thick of things, taking on the leviathan all by herself if she was here. I wouldn't want that."

That surprised Urse. She'd thought, underneath the excellent manners, John wasn't a chauvinist. He was polite and opened doors, and the like, but he didn't seem to think less of the women in town or their abilities. In fact, she'd never felt that he thought less of her power simply because she was female. Urse frowned.

"I thought you'd take any help against the leviathan," she stated, pausing in her meal to await an explanation. He'd better have a good one.

"Normally, I would, but mates are special. I don't even want Red out there, risking himself, but I know him and his abilities. I know he has good judgment and won't take unnecessary risks now, because he's mated, and that means his actions directly affect his mate. If he died here, he'd be breaking her heart, and he knows better than to do that when it can be avoided."

Urse stopped frowning. That did sound like a good reason, but she said nothing, wanting to hear more of his reasoning.

"I don't know his mate, Trisha, at all. I know her brothers, but not her. I can't trust that she wouldn't take one risk too many in seeking to defeat the leviathan, and none of us could back her up. She's a water sprite. She can go right out there in the ocean and battle the creature in its element. None of us can do that. Even if it means we're at risk a little longer here on land, I'd rather wait until her brothers are free to do the job. They, at least, can back each other up, and have years of experience battling things in oceans the world over. From what I've heard, Trisha has lived a much quieter life. At least until she met Red. He told us about their first meeting and all the havoc that followed." John grinned as he resumed eating. "They had a rocky road to mating, and had to fight an evil mage along the way, but they prevailed. I'm happy for them."

That sounded like a story—and really good reasoning for his stance on Trisha not being here. Faith restored, Urse went back to her meal.

"She sounds really interesting." She frowned again as she speared a piece of beef with her fork.

"Yeah, Red got lucky. All the Redstone brothers did, actually. Red was telling us how they all found mates within a year or two of each other. Lucky bastards."

Urse thought how different it was in the shifter world, where mating was considered the ultimate happiness. Many human men would've been saying how sad it was that the five brothers were leg-shackled—or some other unflattering expression. Shifters, she'd discovered, were genuinely happy about others of their kind finding mates and eagerly searched for their own special someone as soon as they hit adulthood.

"If mating is so important to you guys, why are so many of you single?" she asked, curious.

John put down his fork, his demeanor turning serious. "That's because finding one's true mate is a rare thing." He looked straight at her, and she forgot to breathe for a moment. "You see, there's only one for each of us, and we may search our whole lives and never find each other."

"That's really…" Why was she breathless all of a sudden?

"You're mine, Ursula. My mate."

And now her mouth was dry. Was her heart fluttering?

"I'm, um… Really?" She had to clear her throat of the frog that was suddenly there. "I mean… You really think so?"

John got up and walked to her side, taking one of her hands in his and tugged. She rose on unsteady feet to face him.

"I know so. My bear is in agreement. You're mine, Ursula."

Oh, wow. She couldn't speak as he his head descended, his lips capturing hers in a kiss of possession. His dominant Alpha tendencies were on full display, and something inside her melted and wanted to roll over and let him do whatever he wanted. He had that much power over her.

And she knew, without a shadow of a doubt, that he would never abuse his power. Which was why she gave it so freely. He would never hurt her. Never betray her. He would protect her and cherish her the way she yearned to cherish and protect him.

Maybe that's what mating was all about? Could it really be that simple?

A part of her really wanted to believe that it could be so simple. A part that still believed in fairy tales and happily ever after wanted to think that she and John could be together forever.

Dare she believe it? Could she have her happily ever after? Would the other shifters let them?

As the kiss deepened, worries took a back seat to passion. She felt the sensation of movement and found herself deposited on the other end of the long kitchen table, sitting on the edge with her legs splayed and John between them. She mentally cursed the layers of cloth that separated them.

Her desire was an instant burn when it came to John. She'd never responded to any man the way she did to him. Was that because she was his mate? Was he hers? She thought so. If mages could have such beliefs.

But she had a little bit of bear blood in her too. Was it enough to form the bond they'd need if this mating thing was going to work?

BIANCA D'ARC

Goddess, she hoped so, because John was everything she'd ever wanted in a man...and then some. She hadn't ever considered the idea that she might end up married to a shifter, but John had a way of making her want try all sorts of new things.

Such as making love on the kitchen table.

It might not be very hygienic, but she'd make sure to clean up after...if only he could be convinced. She had a feeling it wasn't going to take all that much convincing. Already she could feel the ridge of his erection pressing against her cloth-covered pussy. Oh, yeah. He wanted it too.

She pushed at his clothing, wanting it gone. John obliged by removing his shirt, then hers. Sweet Goddess, he felt good against her. His chest rubbed her nipples in just the right way as their kiss resumed, and went on and on.

She lifted up off the table as best she could while he pulled her pants down and tossed them away. She didn't care where they ended up, or that her ass was bare against the butcher block. She'd clean it later, she promised herself again.

What mattered now was getting John to be as naked as she. Or at least, that very important part of him that she wanted inside her. Now.

John's hands caressed her body, sliding along the insides of her thighs and making her squirm. One hand went around to cup her butt while the other slid closer and closer to her wet folds. He pushed one long, thick finger inside of her.

She couldn't help herself. She moaned.

And then, he added another finger and began a slow rhythm that made her want more. She didn't need any more stimulation, she needed him. Now.

Urse clawed at his shoulders, hoping he would understand. She couldn't form words, even if he'd stopped kissing her long enough for her to utter them.

His finger left her, and she whimpered for its loss. Then she heard the rasp of his zipper and seconds later...

Oh, yeah.

Just what she wanted. He pushed inside her quickly, giving

170

her everything. Giving her himself.

He began to move almost at once, their pace hard and urgent. She was with him, wanting what he wanted, craving more of him until she had it all. She needed him more in that moment than she needed her next breath.

He pushed into her, driving her passion higher as their pace increased. He slammed into her, and she wanted it hard and fast—exactly what he gave her. She squirmed against him, her balance precarious on the end of the table, but she was beyond caring.

At the very last, she came with a shout. And the words she shouted in her delirium echoed through the room.

She'd said...

Oh, Goddess. She'd said she loved him.

CHAPTER FOURTEEN

John was stunned both by the power of his orgasm and the shocking words Ursula cried out as her passion peaked. If his mind wasn't playing tricks and his ears hadn't misheard, she'd said she loved him.

Sweet Mother of All. She loved him.

And he loved her. Goddess, how he loved her.

He buried his face in her neck as they rode out the aftershocks. His knees were weak, but he wasn't about to leave the warm haven of her body. Not until he had to.

"I love you too," he whispered near her ear. "I love you so much, babe. You're my world."

She stiffened a bit, but he wasn't letting go.

"You do?" Her tone was filled with unmistakable wonder, and it gave him hope.

"I really do. Did you mean what you said before? Or was it just the heat of the moment?"

He was giving her an out and praying at the same time that she didn't take it. She paused for a moment before answering, and his whole life flashed before his eyes in that short space of time. The course of the rest of his existence would be set by her reply. It was a significant moment.

"It was, and I did."

"What?" His brain was a little too scrambled from

pleasure to be certain he had the right answers in the correct order.

"It was rather heated passion, and yes, I did mean it." She kissed his jaw as his world started turning again. "I didn't fully realize the depth of my feelings until just now. We've condensed a lot into a few short days. Are you sure..." She took a deep breath, then continued, "Are you sure it's real?"

"It's real," he assured her. "It happens fast for shifters. I've known for a while that you're my perfect mate. I was just hoping you'd feel the same. Or at least that you'd be willing to give us a chance and see where this was leading us."

She smiled, and he could feel it against his throat. "I'm willing. Or hadn't you noticed?"

He chuckled. "I noticed. And I already thanked the Goddess for sending me a mate as perfect for me as you." He nibbled on her ear. "I love you, Ursula."

He lifted her off the table, his hands under her butt and walked her down the hallway, his cock coming back to life, still inside her, as he moved. She gasped at every sensation. There John went again, getting her to try something new. She'd never been with a man strong enough to carry her while they were joined together.

He walked them straight through his bedroom and into the master bath. By the time he had them inside the massive shower, she was ready to come again. Each step he'd taken had rubbed the head of his hard cock up against something inside her that made her want to explode in ecstasy.

John pressed her up against the tiled wall, and she didn't even feel the chill of the marble against her back. Nothing could penetrate the haze of pleasure he'd built up again so quickly. Only a few more thrusts and she was singing his name as she came again, her body convulsing around his as he joined her.

After long moments of shared bliss, he reached over and turned on the shower. When he finally parted their bodies, she was glad he'd thought to bring them directly in here. She was dripping with his come.

What had been incredibly naughty during the encounter was now sticky and somewhat uncomfortable. But John seemed to understand. He bathed her with a soft sponge and gentle herbal soap that had a fresh scent that wasn't overpowering. He reached up into places that made her squirm and spent time tickling other places on her body that made her giggle.

She splashed him with water, and he directed the showerheads to tease her into a renewed interest. After he'd cleaned her and dried her off with a fluffy, heated towel, he carried her back into his bedroom and lay her down on the freshly made bed.

They made love long into the night, and when the sun rose, she stayed in bed, too tired to move, while he rose. Between the sex and the magic expenditure of the night before—and what was to come when the moon rose—she needed her sleep.

*

When she finally woke from an exhausted sleep, Urse was groggy. She could hear voices coming from the main part of the house. She roused herself enough to take a quick shower, put on fresh clothes, and make her way into the main part of the house.

Cam was there. She wasn't surprised to see him. She figured the fey knight would want to go over the plans for the evening's magical work—the grandest to date. Urse rolled her shoulders, trying to ease the tension that crept in when she allowed herself to think about what was coming.

This would be the biggest challenge of her magical life.

She just had to keep believing that her grandmother would never set a task before her that she couldn't handle. Urse had no doubt that it would be difficult, but she had to have faith that she could do it. She had to proceed as if success was inevitable. That was going to be her inner mantra for the rest of the evening.

She padded into the living room in only her socks, but she knew darn well that John was aware of every step she took. She was learning that shifter hearing was even more acute than she had thought. When he turned and smiled at her, her breath caught. The man was temptation and sin, all rolled up into a hunky package that she wanted to open again and again.

Like they had last night.

That naughty thought sent a flush of heat to her cheeks. John winked at her, making her blush even hotter. The devil somehow knew exactly what she'd been thinking—or if not her exact thoughts, then something darn close.

"Ah, Lady Ursula, it's good to see you looking so well rested." Cam spoke as if he didn't see a byplay between herself and John.

"It's just Urse, please," she invited as she took a seat near John. They were gathered in the living room, a pot of coffee on the low table in front of the couch and several empty mugs. "Are you expecting more company?" She looked significantly at the empty, clean coffee cups and the full pot.

"Some of the lads are outside checking the perimeter. They'll be along shortly," Cam told her. "I just wanted a few words with the Alpha, and now that we've done that, and you're awake, we can get on with tonight's business."

Urse was intrigued by the idea that the fey knight had wanted a private word with John. What could they have been talking about? And why would it be necessary to keep whatever was a secret from the rest of John's men?

Urse had seen the group in action and quickly realized that John didn't hold many secrets from his men—at least not for long. The biggest thing he'd ever not told them about was his idea for the town itself. From all accounts, he'd bided his time, quietly preparing until they were ready to retire. That's when he'd finally revealed his plans to the guys.

But she was certain he would never have concealed something harmful. If one of the men had found out, somehow, that he'd been buying up land in the Pacific Northwest and asked him why, John would have told them all about his idea much sooner. He would never have lied to them. It simply wasn't the way he led. And she would bet her bottom dollar, his guys wouldn't tolerate subterfuge or dishonesty in anyone they worked with—especially not someone they had honored with the title of Alpha.

So it couldn't be anything bad. John simply wouldn't allow key information to be withheld from his team. That only deepened the mystery as far as Urse was concerned.

What could Cam possibly have to say to John that fit that criteria?

One thing was perfectly clear. She wouldn't be hearing about it today from either of them.

Sighing, she let it go, reaching forward to pour herself a cup of coffee. Almost at the exact moment she sat back to take a sip, the front door opened and the Chambers brothers came in.

Brody, the sheriff, and Jack, who acted as Game Warden, were cut very much of the same cloth. Both tall. Both rugged. Both handsome and polite. But where Brody was more talkative and friendly—and much better with people, in general—Jack was more reserved.

From what Urse had seen in her weeks in town, Jack almost never socialized or spent much time on Main Street, where all the businesses were located. She'd seen his official vehicle drive through many times, but he never really got out and walked around. She supposed his work kept him busy in the great outdoors, and he was probably more comfortable with silence than with conversation.

Even as they sat down on the couch, it was Brody who leaned forward, making small talk and giving John his report, while Jack leaned back, simply observing. He was a quiet one. Nothing wrong with that, Urse thought. But she wondered if the old adage was true about still waters running deep.

The door opened again, and the three visiting shifters came in, followed by Deputy Zak. Each acknowledged her with a nod or a brief hello, then grabbed whatever space was available around the coffee table. Some sat on the floor. Joe Nightwing perched on an armrest, somewhat predictably, she thought, seeing as how he was a bird shifter.

Before long, they had a cozy group, all drinking coffee like it was going out of style and looking to John to start the briefing. She wondered what he was going to say too. She'd been asleep all day while he'd been up, doing things and learning what effect her work of the night before had had on the cove.

John started by giving everyone a clear picture of what had happened during the day. He'd been collecting all the *intel*, as he called it—the various reports from everyone who was noticing changes and reporting them to him. It occurred to her then that he was acting as the information collection point. He was sorting through the various streams of data from everyone out in the field and putting together the big picture. From that, he was designing strategy tailor made to deal with various problems that had cropped up.

For example, the few fishing boats that called the cove home had come back with observations that might have meant nothing individually, but in aggregate created a picture of a calm zone in the ocean extending from the northern tip of the cove, where they'd been last night, for about a mile in all directions. Urse was seriously impressed. She hadn't really thought she'd have that much reach with her spell, but then again, she'd never really been in tune with someone the way she was now with John.

Because of their new harmony, her ability to draw on his magic—and that of those he was connected to—had been a lot easier than even just the day before. Perhaps that new ease between them had allowed her to push the boundaries of her spell much farther than she'd never expected.

Then there was Cam. The fey knight's contribution couldn't really be calculated. At least not by Urse. Only Cam really knew what effect he was having on her spellwork.

It seemed the fey liked being a mystery. She supposed it

was in the nature of the beast. Fey hadn't been known as tricksters and magicians the world over for centuries for no reason. He'd acted as a distraction to the leviathan last night, when she'd needed one most, but she really had no idea if he had contributed his own brand of magic to somehow bolster her work.

Whatever the cause, Urse was damn impressed, if she did say so herself. Oh, she wasn't going to get the big head over this. She also knew full well that she could never have done anything even remotely that big alone. It was the combination of magics, and the willingness of the bear shifters to lend her their strength through their Alpha, that had made it possible.

That was a rare convergence of events. After tonight, it would probably never be repeated in her lifetime. At least she was hoping that would be the case, because wielding such magics was both exhausting and dangerous—and she would only do it in the most dire of circumstances.

She prayed they would never face another situation so extreme that she would have to call upon John and his men to lend her their power. If they could do that, they might just have a shot at a peaceful life here in the cove.

As the briefing went on, John painted a picture of success tempered by the need for more action. The leviathan was on the move. The lone, brave fisherman who'd dared to take his boat out beyond the safe zone had described a roiling sea, filled with evil creatures like the one that had attacked Zak's mate in the cove not too long ago.

While the new wards seemed to be keeping the creatures off shore in the three areas that had already been warded, they could, and were, still gathering in deeper waters and the non-warded area. So the water was still off limits to everyone, and would be for some time to come. Urse wasn't too concerned about that. The water was going to be Mellie's problem. Urse was concentrating on the land. Though, of course, she would offer her sister all the support and help she needed when the time came.

The important thing for right now was to protect everyone

on land as best as she could. That was her mission, and that's what she would finish—to the very best of her abilities—tonight. Goddess willing.

When talk turned to where the men would be stationed around the area where they would be working and the coffee pot ran empty, Urse got up to make a new pot. She didn't really need to know every single detail of where every man would be. She trusted to John to deploy his people and see to their safety. That was his thing, by all accounts, strategizing who would work best where.

No, Urse had to focus on her part in all of this. She was going to be the one on stage, as it were, though every man who was backing them up played an important part. She couldn't do what had to be done without them, but by the same token, she didn't want to flub her part and screw everything up at the last minute.

So she needed some alone time to think and prepare quietly.

Currently, that was the kitchen. She reloaded the coffee maker with fresh ground coffee and simply stood there, watching it perk. The steam rose from the back of the machine in little whispers that were almost hypnotic. Perfect. Just what she needed to take the stress off her shoulders for a couple of minutes.

She watched the steam and blanked her mind, looking within to settle her stretched nerves. She was peripherally aware of someone walking into the kitchen a few minutes later, and she blinked, breaking the mini-meditative session. She breathed deeply, enjoying the aroma of fresh coffee as it wafted through the kitchen. Even just those few minutes away from the stress in the other room had refreshed her.

She turned her head to face the newcomer into her private space and was unsurprised to find Cam leaning sideways against the kitchen counter, his arms folded in front of him as he watched her. He smiled, and something in the twinkle of his eye said he knew exactly what she'd been doing.

"Welcome back," he said, nodding toward her in a playful

way. "Smart of you to take a little break from the testosterone convention out there."

She sniffed at him, playing along. "As if you're not part of it. You're as bad as the rest of them."

He bowed his head in acknowledgment. "Ask me no questions, and I'll tell you no lies."

"It wasn't a question. It was a statement of fact." She reached for the pot of coffee, switching off the machine that had finished its job for the moment. She'd bring the whole pot out to the guys, and she was pretty sure it would all be gone before it had time to grow tepid.

"I stand corrected." He didn't move when she made a motion forward.

He wasn't exactly blocking her in a hostile way, but it was pretty clear he wanted to speak to her. She placed the carafe of coffee back on the warmer and turned to face the fey warrior, copying his stance and leaning her hip against the kitchen counter.

"Spit it out." She thought a slight challenge was in order. He seemed to like battling verbally, and being Italian, the fine art of argument—not in an angry way—was her forte.

"Ah, the direct approach. Just like your ol' granny."

Cam smiled at her again, and she had to stop herself from reacting to the reminder that he was the next best thing to immortal and had known her Nonna as a young woman. It was a strange feeling, dealing with a fey. Even weirder was the juxtaposition of his role as knight protector and this wise ass side of him that was all troublesome male. Who was the real Cameron? Would she ever get to know him well enough to know what his real personality was? Or did she even want to get that close to a fey?

After all, he would never grow old. Perhaps this standoffishness on his part was a protective defense. If everyone he befriended eventually died and he just kept going, that had to be hard on his heart. Losing friends was always hard. Maybe he'd decided to keep everyone at arm's length as a way to prevent the pain of loss.

Unfortunately, she didn't think that was going to work out for him. No matter how hard you tried, you could never completely shut out the world from your heart. Not if you were a good person. And there was no doubt in her mind that Cam was good. He would never have been blessed by the Goddess to be one of Her chosen knights if he wasn't pure of heart.

So the cocky attitude had to be a defense mechanism. She couldn't really blame him, though it was a little annoying.

"What's on your mind, Cam?"

He seemed to study her for a moment before replying. He squinted a bit, tilting his head as if examining a specimen under a microscope.

"I wanted to be sure you were in the right frame of mind for tonight's work. It's all well and good for the bears out there to come up with an action plan, but you're the one on whom everything will rise or fall. Your role cannot be underestimated, and your emotional state is crucial." His expression lightened just a tiny bit. "So, tell me, how are you feeling?"

"Truthfully?" She dropped her head, looking up at him from the side, allowing her shoulders to slump a bit. "Tired." She rolled her head around, trying to loosen the kinks in her neck. "I've never done this much sustained magic in my life. And I've never handled so much raw power. The bears…"

"They pack a wallop, don't they?" Cam agreed, smiling kindly. "Furry little buggers."

She had to chuckle at that ridiculous description of the mighty grizzlies and their assorted friends who sat in the other room and, even now, she knew, guarded the perimeter of their Alpha's land. There was nothing *little* about any of them. Not their size, nor their magical power. Each and every one of them was formidable on every level.

"I suspect only a fey could get away with saying that."

"And only out of earshot. Aye, you're right, lass." Cam kept the mood between them convivial. "And how are you doing with the Alpha? Are things settled between you?"

"Settled?" She had to think about that for a moment. "We have feelings for each other, but I'm not sure how his people will react to it. Frankly, I'm worried they'll still want to run me and my sister out of town after this is all over." She slumped against the counter a bit more. "We come from such different traditions. I keep wondering if a shifter and a *strega* can really make a go of it."

Cam seemed to study her before saying quietly, "Francisco and Violetta did, and the world was a better place for them in it."

That sounded as if…

"Did you know them?" She had to ask, though the very thought of it boggled her mind.

Cam sighed. "Aye. I knew your ancestors and called them friends. They would both be very proud of what you're doing here, and I think Francisco, in particular, would've liked your Alpha. They are cut very much of the same cloth."

This was a rare opportunity. Cam had been there. He'd seen how her ancestors interacted, the challenges they'd faced, the way they'd managed such a diverse relationship. She could pick his brain…if he let her.

"How did they do it?" she asked simply, hoping he'd give her some clue, some hope.

"That would be telling." Cam's eyes twinkled as he grinned, and she couldn't believe he was teasing her now, about something so very important.

She growled at him, surprising herself a bit. She'd never growled at someone before. Maybe John was rubbing off on her more than she knew.

Cam straightened away from the counter and gazed at her, approval in his eyes.

"Now that, right there, is why you'll probably have an easier time of it than they did. You have Francisco's blood in your veins. The others will recognize it on some level, if they haven't already. The more you are around John and his people, the more you will feel the influence. Oh, you'll never be a bear shifter, but you're an Alpha female in your own right. That ought to go a long way toward solving any problems that might crop up."

"I'm not that strong," Urse insisted, almost afraid to believe what he said might be true. It meant so much to her that John's people accept their relationship. She didn't want to cause a rift between him and his comrades.

"Being an Alpha female is more than the kind of strength you're probably talking about. Being a true Alpha female means being like the Goddess—kind and benevolent when needed, nurturing all in Her path, being there for anyone who needs help, but also steadfast when necessary, as you are being now in placing your wards. You are already caring for the Clan gathered here by doing so. They recognize it. You'll see. You're earning their respect with everything you do here, lass." Cam's expression was serious. She almost believed him. "And if you canna believe me..." he said, as if reading her mind, "...then have a talk with Steve before he leaves. Ask him about his mother. Now there was an Alpha female of the highest caliber, Goddess bless her."

Cam walked closer and put his hands on both of her shoulders. He was a lot taller than she was—taller even than John—so she felt tiny and sort of enclosed by his presence. His gaze held hers, and the space between them became charged with a benevolent sort of energy.

"You must put all these thoughts from your mind tonight, lass. You have to focus your mind, body, heart and soul on the spell. Only then, will you succeed in protecting this place and its people."

She felt every word as if it were an imperative, etched in her mind. Was he using some kind of magic on her? She wasn't sure, but did it really matter? It was for good. He was a knight, pledged to the Goddess Herself. She trusted him.

And as she thought that, the magic he had been using absorbed into her skin, into her body, mind, and soul. Probably just as he'd intended. And she could feel the goodness. This was his way of helping her.

Cam smiled at her. "I wish I could do more for ye, lassie,

but this is your trial. Your task. I do not doubt you. See that you do not doubt yourself."

She smiled back at him. "I'll do my best."

"Aye." He dropped his hands and stepped back. "That is all we can ever ask of ourselves."

Cam moved away, toward the entrance to the kitchen, and that's when Urse saw John standing there, in the archway. He was frowning at Cam, but the fey merely smiled and sauntered out of the room.

John moved inside and walked closer to her.

"You okay?" he asked, still frowning.

She went right up to him and put her arms around his waist, hugging him close and resting her cheek against his chest.

John wasn't sure what to make of the scene he had just walked in on, but having Urse in his arms felt good. Good enough for him to not go after the fey bastard who had just been way too close to his mate.

"I'm good, John," she said softly, her words muffled against his chest. "In fact, when I'm with you, I'm the best I've ever been."

His breath caught. She'd just hit the nail on the head of feelings he'd been having for a while now, but couldn't quite articulate. There was something about having Urse in his life that made him a better man. A better leader. A better Alpha.

"Roger that, honey, and right back at'cha," he whispered, bending his head so that he could kiss the crown of her hair.

They stood there, content in each other's arms for long moments. Only the arrival of Zak, looking for fresh coffee, broke them apart. Zak stole the carafe from the warming plate and went back out into the living room, but by then, John and Urse had let go of each other, though they didn't go far. Arm in arm, they walked back into the living room to face the knowing looks of the rest of the team.

Nobody said anything for a moment until finally Zak broke the tension by the simple act of pouring more coffee for everyone. Eventually, he sat back down in his spot around the low table, and they all got back to work.

John felt like roaring with Urse tucked close to his side as the guys kept right on making plans. None of them objected, which meant they tacitly approved of the relationship. It was a good omen for breaking the news to everyone.

But that could wait until after the ceremony tonight. Actually, it could wait until John and Urse were damn good and ready to talk about their mating.

CHAPTER FIFTEEN

Long before the moon rose, everyone was in position. John had taken Urse to a spot she never would have expected on the southern tip of the cove. On a rocky bluff stood a short circle of stones. A sacred place.

Oh, it wasn't Stonehenge. The rocks here were smaller and uncut. They looked more like the standing stones in France than the more orderly blocks of England, but they would get the job done. This felt like a natural formation, put here when the earth was young, blessed of the Goddess.

The circle itself had a small diameter. It was only a few yards across at its widest point, but the energy of the place was powerful. Wild. Untamed. And intense.

Urse caught her breath the moment she walked inside the small ring. John was right beside her. Steadying her.

"Yeah, I was wondering how you were going to take that. This place..." His words were low, not carrying out beyond the circle. "I have a buddy who's a shaman. He lives near here, and he's been keeping an eye on this circle. It's not quite ready for the uninitiated yet, he tells me. How is it for you?"

Urse breathed shallowly. "I'll be okay. Just let me get my bearings."

She reached out for the nearest of the standing stones, which was about at waist height. Touching the rock, she felt its hum of power straight down to her toes. It was unlike anything she'd ever felt before.

"Best way to do it." She heard Cam's comment as if from far away.

He was standing beside John, watching her. When had he arrived? She wasn't sure. She'd been too overwhelmed by the hum of magical energy contained in the ring to be aware of much else.

She saw Cam frowning and realized he'd asked her something.

"What?" She shook her head, but all she heard was the hum of the ring in her mind.

She saw Cam reach out to touch the standing stone nearest him. The hum increased, but then settled down. Words came to her. Cam's words, though she was looking right at him and his mouth didn't open once.

"Control it, lass. Do not get swept up in it. Form it to your will." He did something, manipulating the energy. "Like this."

He showed her the way, teaching her something she never could have put into words. He taught by example, how to take the power of the ring into herself and shape it to what she needed, subduing it to do as she wished. It was truly amazing.

Within a few minutes, she had learned how to control it, though she never could have imagined such a thing only an hour ago. She hadn't known such places held so much raw energy. The only stone circles she'd ever been to had been well regulated by use and time...which made her think.

"This is new, isn't it?" she asked Cam as the power dialed back to something she could handle.

"Aye. This ring cropped up probably about the same time the bears moved in. Such things do still happen once in a very long while. The concentration of shifter magic probably caused this to form, a benevolent outcropping to concentrate power they could use—if any were so gifted."

They were speaking aloud now, and the background noise filtered back in. Her senses were returning to normal as she regulated the flow of raw energy back to something she could handle.

"That's why Gus, the shaman, chose to live nearby," John told them. "He's heavily involved with the native community to the south, and when this place is ready, he'll act on our behalf as well. He's got a foot in both worlds. I wish he were here for this, but he's back east at the moment."

"I think she's got the hang of it now," Cam said, looking at Urse but speaking to John. "Judging by the sky, and the sea, we should probably start getting ready." Cam nodded toward the disturbance in the ocean, clearly heading their way.

John whistled, and the men just outside the stone circle stepped in. Tonight, everyone would be inside the ring of protection afforded by the standing stones. Urse wouldn't have to cast a ring in salt. Not when a much more formidable circle, formed of the earth itself, was already there to shield them.

Her full attention and energy could be focused on forming the spell and wielding the power of their combined magics at the enemy. This would be the most powerful spell of all. Probably the most powerful she would ever be called upon to make in her life. She vowed to make it a good one. It would be her master work.

The men took up positions in a circle, just inside the circle of stones. They faced the center of the ring, where she, John and Cam were standing in a triangle, back to back, shoulder to shoulder, facing outward. Urse faced the ocean. John faced the cove. And Cam had the edge of the triangle facing the land. He was their support, guarding the rear while she and John faced the threat head on. As it should be.

Through the circle of men and stones, she could see the ocean roiling with anger as the creatures within it—the evil one and its minions—let loose their rage. It was a mighty sight, designed, she believed, to strike terror into her heart. But she wasn't so easily scared. Not after her success with the three spells that had gone before.

This would be the most demanding yet, but she also had the best setup she'd ever had. Powerful shifters all around her, willing to guard her and lend her some of their magic. Plus the wild magic of the newly-formed ring of standing stones, pushed up from Mother Earth in response to the magical creatures living nearby, probably for just such a purpose.

If she understood her early lessons on such things correctly, the ancient rings were formed to help the magical races focus their power and give them ceremonial places. Places to marry. Places to celebrate life and death. Places to seek shelter and understanding. Places to increase their own power to use for good works.

Well, this had to be the biggest good work Urse would ever attempt. The three spells that had gone before had been powerful, but with the light of the full moon and the input of the shifters, the fey and the presence of the stones... She figured this final spell was going to be a doozy.

She just hoped she lived through it.

Either way though, she would see it set. If she had to give up her life to protect the people of this place and deny the sea monster any further incursion on this land, then so be it. Her only regret was leaving John. And her sister. Both would be crushed if she left them, but they would also understand why she did what she was about to do.

Because unbeknownst to either of them, the ward she was going to cast tonight was going to take all her power...and then some.

Cam knew. She had seen the knowledge in his eyes as they were making their plans. If she was reading him right, even he wasn't sure the combined powers that were being lent to her tonight would be enough to keep her from flaming out. She had no idea, but they were about to find out.

The moon had been up for a while, raining its powerful light down on the stones. It was so bright there was no need for additional lights. Everything was lit by the moon's reflected light for miles and miles all around. It was beautiful, but it was also a thrumming beat in Urse's blood.

The moon was an aspect of the Goddess worshiped the world over in centuries past. And for good reason. Her Light was powerful when the moon showed her full face.

"Now, lass," Cam whispered behind her. "The moon nears its peak."

All this time, Urse had been quietly gathering her power…and her courage. She felt the build-up, pulsing through the earth at the center of the circle, just below her feet. The power was frightening, but she wasn't scared. She felt a calm come over her as she invoked the Goddess, starting her chant that would form the ward she'd spent a lifetime learning how to cast.

This was the greatest spell she knew. The greatest spell she would ever cast, if she was lucky. It would take everything within and without to make this work.

But she wasn't alone. The Goddess was with her. And her mate was with her too. And Cam. Quiet, blessed, supportive Cam. A new friend who went back with her family, almost to its beginning.

She saw it all in those brief moments when the power coalesced in her. She felt the individual magics of the shifters gathered all around. Many bears, but also the great horned owl spirit of Joe Nightwing and the golden jackal of Seth. The mighty cougar that shared Steve Redstone's soul blinked at her from Steve's eyes where he faced her in the protective inner ring.

She glanced at all the men and saw the shadow of their beast halves. If she looked close enough, she could see their souls.

That was a knowledge she didn't necessarily want to have, but was bestowed on her by the Mother of All in the timeless moments between one word of her chanted prayer and the next. Time had slowed. The angry flailing of the evil creatures in the ocean went into slow motion as Urse spun out her spell, each word dragging a new aspect of her magic, and the ward she wanted to build, out of her being, with the support and power of those gathered around.

She could feel it. The ward was taking shape, but her power was failing. She'd bit off more than she could chew. Panic gripped her for a split second...

And then, John was there. He'd reached behind him to take her hand, and his calm strength flowed into her.

Then Cam followed suit on her other side, taking her other hand. The power that flowed into her was the golden Light of the Goddess Herself, nearly overwhelming in its intensity.

Then she knew. It was time.

She raised her hands—John and Cam's hands too— toward the sky, and the power poured forth, racing up to the moon and ricocheting back down to the cove and the surrounding waters.

The leviathan screamed an inhuman sound, unable to withstand the searing magic. It fought against the goodness of Urse's spell with its own evil magic. The smell of ozone filled the air as energy clashed in the air all around them.

Urse felt her hair lifting, forming a halo around her head as the magic battle generated a massive static electricity charge. The stones of the circle glowed as the evil tried to overcome the Goddess's ring of protection.

Urse poured on the power, calling on the men all around, Cam's seemingly limitless strength, and finally, the earth itself. Giving all she had of her own energy, Urse screamed the final words of her chant, sealing the spell with the last of her strength.

The moon glowed brighter for a moment, and then, the lightning was released. The static charge reversed and went from the land to the sea, lighting up the leviathan and hundreds and hundreds of smaller evil creatures that flanked it in an army of tentacles and menace.

But it was an army that was on the run.

Urse gasped as she got a good look at what was in the water. Lightning danced over and inside the waves, lighting the water from below, giving everyone a good look at the sheer magnitude of the enemy.

She was glad she hadn't known how many were out there before she'd started setting her wards. Even now, she couldn't quite believe the sheer numbers of unearthly creatures the leviathan had managed to rouse for its water-bound army of darkness.

With her last conscious thought, Urse smiled. She could see the boundaries of her ward. They extended even farther than she had hoped. The leviathan and its minions were fleeing as fast as they could move, and the odor of burnt seaweed and ozone filled the air.

"Honey?" John's voice came to her as she started to sink, letting go of his and Cam's hands. Her strength was gone. Given gladly in service to the Light, in setting a permanent ward that would protect this land and coast for generations to come.

"Love you," she whispered, even as John's arms came around her. He held her tight against his chest, and she was glad. She wanted her last thought to be of him. Her last moments to be with him.

John felt the breath leave Urse's body, and his bear roared in his skull. John was hit with a jolt of pain as he'd never felt before. His mate was dying?

No way would he allow that.

John turned angry, glowing eyes on the fey.

"Cam?"

"Put her down on the ground and stand back," Cam instructed, looking weary but determined. "Your lass gave her all for this place, but if I have anything to say, she will not leave it this easily." Cam looked up at the circle of shifters who were all gazing at them with concern. "Hold your positions and join hands. Pray as you have never prayed before for this selfless woman who was willing to give her life so that you all could be safe." Cam's impassioned words were fast and filled with emotion, which John saw repeated on every face of every man around the circle.

John dropped to his knees, placing Urse's near-lifeless body on the ground in the center of the circle. He lifted her hand to his lips and kissed it, beseeching the Mother of All to take him instead. If someone had to leave this realm, he prayed, let it be him, so that Urse might live. She was too good to let pass this way. Too loved. Too kind.

Cam stood on the other side and began to whisper words of high magic. John couldn't hear exactly what the elf said, nor did he really care. All that mattered to him in the world was lying before him on the ground, pale and growing cold.

He felt the tears falling down his face and knew he was crying for perhaps the first time since childhood, but he didn't care. His mate—his *mate*—wasn't in her body where she was supposed to be. He wanted her back. He *needed* her back!

He lifted his face to the sky and allowed the bear to roar its agony out of his mouth. Both halves of his soul were in mortal pain.

And then, the earth moved.

John felt the earth beneath his knees tremble and heard it groan, and then, the hand he was holding—Urse's hand— rose in his grip. He looked down again to try to figure out what was going on. Was she getting up? Was she alive?

But it wasn't her moving. It was the ground itself.

A slab of rock was rising. An *altar* was rising. In the center of the sacred stone circle, an alter of living rock rose to their call, answering their prayers. John knelt on one side, Cam stood on the other, his hands outstretched, his body glowing with the magical armor of his calling.

John didn't question it. A Knight of the Light was bringing forth the magic of the earth. He was expending his energy to try to save John's mate. John had no doubt that if the Goddess willed it, Urse could come back to him.

It would be a miracle of the highest caliber, but John had to believe that the Goddess he had served all his life would not break his heart. She would not have brought them together only to part them so soon.

Would she?

John stood as the altar kept rising. The stones of the circle, too, seemed to grow from the short stumps they'd been into taller, more defined standing stones. And they were glowing, swirling with energy in a slightly different way than they had when Urse had used their power in her ward.

The colors were different. Before it had been pure white, icy moonlight. Now it was green and gold, the colors of forest and fey, earth and sun. Cam's golden armor shone with the same pure gold light.

And as John watched, the altar lit up, surrounding Urse's limp body in the same golden glow, tinged with the grey and brown of the earth and the green of growing things. The glow bathed her body, filling it and bringing color back to her cheeks, and finally, as a blue wisp of magic from the sky came into play...air back to her lungs.

She was alive.

Dear, sweet Mother of All. Urse was alive!

CHAPTER SIXTEEN

Urse woke in John's house. In John's bed. But John wasn't there.

She sensed him though. He was just outside, in the living room, with Cam and the three shifters he'd brought to town. How exactly she knew that, she didn't quite know, but she was aware that things had changed for her.

In a rush, everything that had happened at the stone circle came back to her.

Judging from the sunlight behind the curtains, it was daytime. She knew her ward was set. She'd seen that with her own eyes before she collapsed.

And then…

Urse sat bolt upright in the bed, then grabbed her forehead. *Damn.* She had a hangover. Or something that felt a lot like it.

She gingerly swung her legs over the side of the bed. She was dressed in loose pajamas. Fleece. They were hers, from her apartment. Somehow she knew that Mel had brought them over, but was no longer in John's house.

Mel had been in the room though. She'd checked on Urse, which touched her greatly. Her little sister was the best. Even when she was being pesky, she always meant well. Urse loved that about her.

Judging herself presentable enough, Urse padded in sock feet toward the hall that would lead her to the living room...and her mate. Mmm. She wanted nothing more than to see John and get one of those hugs that made her feel as if nothing bad would ever happen to her as long as he held her in his arms.

John heard his mate walking down the hallway and moved to intercept. He'd worried over her deep sleep, but Cam had assured him, over and over, that she'd be fine after she slept off the effects of her power expenditure.

The guys had finally convinced him to leave her side by sending the visitors to him bearing gifts—a gourmet meal packed in to-go containers. His men were guarding the perimeter, but they knew John wouldn't snub the visitors by telling them to take a hike. Not when Steve Redstone was in the group. Or the Jackal. Or Joe Nightwing. Or Cam, for that matter.

All three shifters were strong Alphas, and Cam... Well, Cam was something akin to an angelic being as far as John was concerned, now that he'd seen the Knight of the Light in action.

John went into the hall, running into Urse and catching her in his arms. She wound herself around him, snuggling close.

"This is just what I wanted. A bear hug," she whispered, her face against his chest.

"How are you feeling?" He couldn't express the relief that flooded him just knowing she was alive and coherent. And standing! He hadn't expected that so soon.

"Like I've got the hangover from hell. Don't talk above a whisper, and we should be fine. Do I smell coffee?" She didn't move from his arms, for which he was grateful. She was in a lazy, kittenish sort of mood that suited him just fine.

With every word she spoke, he began to believe that she would come out of her near-death experience unscathed. Goddess be praised.

"Yeah, the guys sent food over. I sort of refused to leave your side."

"Well, good for them for looking out for you. And I love that you stuck by me." She lifted her head long enough to place a little kiss on his cheek. "But you really have to look after yourself too. You have to eat, John."

"So do you. Are you hungry at all?" He liked that she worried about him, but she was the patient here, not him.

"Hmm." She seemed to think about it. "Yeah, I could eat. That was some night last night, huh?"

"Last night?" John took her by the shoulders and drew back so he could look into her eyes. "Honey, that was two days ago. You've been asleep for almost sixty hours."

Stunned disbelief entered her eyes slowly. Her reaction times were off, but then, she'd been dead for a good few minutes there, just two and a half days ago. She had a right to be a little sluggish.

"Seriously?"

He nodded, releasing his grip on her shoulders to rub her arms lightly. He was so glad to be touching her. Talking with her. It was a miracle he would never take for granted.

"Seriously. I brought you here after the moon ceremony and haven't left your side. Cam's been here off and on too. He kept telling me you just had to sleep it off, but I didn't truly believe him until just now. How do you feel?" He knew he was gushing a little, but the cautious joy inside him demanded expression.

"Like I said, hungover. And very sensitive." Her brow drew together in a little frown. "I could tell who was in the house from inside your room. And I knew Mellie had been there, but wasn't in the house any longer."

"She left about an hour ago, when the guys showed up with the food. She said she was leaving me in good hands." He was intrigued by what Urse was describing. "Who do you think is here?"

"Cam, Joe, Steve and Seth," she answered, without hesitation.

"On the nose," he told her, bending to place a little kiss on the tip of her nose.

He was interested in why she could suddenly know things about who was where, when she apparently couldn't before, but it might just be a temporary side effect. Cam had warned him that she might be a little different for the first week or so after she woke up. It was to be expected, he'd said rather mysteriously.

John was too happy to just have her up and around and speaking coherently to delve further into the phenomenon now. If it lasted, he'd ask her more about it later. If not, it wouldn't matter anyway.

What mattered most in this moment was that she was here. She was alive. And she was in his arms. Everything else could wait.

He held her as time stood still, offering a silent prayer of thanks that she was alive, here, now, in his arms, where she belonged. They had both been forever changed by the ordeal they'd been through, and only time would reveal the full extent of the change.

But it was all good, as far as John was concerned. He'd come out of this adventure with a beautiful, smart and talented mate who would make his life fuller and happier than it had ever been. His people not only accepted her, but respected her abilities with a fervor that bordered on awe in some cases. She had pushed back a monster that none of them had ever even contemplated. She had done something none of them was capable of doing, giving of herself—almost too much—in the process. She had earned their esteem, and their love.

"One thing I'm still wondering about." Urse spoke softly as she drew back a short way to look up at him.

"What's that, honey?" He could deny her nothing. If she asked for the moon and stars, he'd start working on a way to get them for her.

"The other day when you and Cam had your little private meeting. What was the big secret? What did you guys talk about?"

"Hmm." He thought about what he could divulge. "Well, I can't tell you everything because I promised Cam I wouldn't until after certain events had happened, but I think it's safe to tell you that Cam is gathering intel from multiple sources, including someone—and I don't know exactly who his source is—that can see the future. One of the things he told me, though to be honest, although it made me happy, it didn't matter as much as he thought it might, is that our children will be able to shift."

She placed one of her hands over his heart, happy surprise clear on her lovely face. "They will? I mean... We're going to have children? Plural? More than one?"

"Apparently so," he agreed, covering her hand with his, holding her touch close to his heart. "It was foreseen that we would have cubs who could shift and would have a lot more magic than most bears." Cam had specifically told John that he could share this bit of intel with Urse, so he wasn't breaking any confidences.

"I'm glad, though I hadn't really thought about it with everything else that was going on," she said, her gaze soft. "I like children."

"I like you, my mate," he echoed her words, smiling. "In fact, I love you, Urse, with everything I am. You make my life whole." His voice dropped as the declaration left his mouth. The moment felt incredibly special.

"I love you too. And if I could see the future right now, I'd predict a happy, love-filled life together for the rest of our days." She smiled, reaching both of her hands around his neck and drawing his head downward for a kiss.

"I like the sound of that," he whispered against her lips, smiling as he deepened the contact and kissed his mate.

The times ahead might be interesting and unpredictable, but he knew now that they could face just about anything...as long as they were together.

He wasn't at liberty yet to tell her everything Cam and he had discussed the day before her final spell, but that was okay, for now. Nothing Cam had said would hurt her in any way, and all would be revealed in time. Cam had taken John into his confidence, showing a respect John had never expected, but was honored to receive from the fey knight.

John's Army days might be behind him, but his mind was already working out strategies based on the information Cam had shared. Strategic planning was John's talent, his avocation and his sharpest skill. He was pleased to be able to use all his training and experience in the battle everyone was expecting would soon be coming to the mortal world.

The past few days had brought John into a small group of those who were actively planning to fight the evil that was working against them. Although he'd come to Grizzly Cove to retire and start a family, he found that he couldn't quite turn his back on the danger that was, in all likelihood, headed their way.

The leviathan might be only the tip of the iceberg. In which case, John couldn't ignore the protective instincts inside him that had pushed him into the military so many years ago. He was a man of action, and of duty. He had skills he had to use to help the world stay free of evil. If he simply shut himself off from the outside world and hid up here in Grizzly Cove, he wouldn't be able to look himself in the mirror each morning.

When Cam had asked him to put his talents to work once again, collating intel from all over the world and devising strategies, John couldn't in all good conscience, say no. On the contrary, his bear prodded him to get back in the game—if only in this small way. He wouldn't be fighting on the front lines unless, and until, they needed him, but he could easily use his brain power and experience on behalf of the good guys.

A conduit was open now between Grizzly Cove and the outside world. Things had changed. The town could no longer hide in obscurity. The leviathan's presence had outed them, for lack of a better description, to the Others in the area. Their secret was no longer a secret, and they'd have to deal with the repercussions of that in the coming days, John was sure, but he was still proud of the town he had helped build. He knew his people could handle what was coming. They were all highly capable and Ursula's contribution these past days could not be discounted. She'd given her all to help protect them, which would come in handy now that they were on the supernatural map, so to speak.

John might have retired from active duty, founded the town that had been his pet project for decades, and even found a powerful, smart and incredibly sexy mate. In fact, he'd met all his goals—something he never expected to happen this soon, or this easily. Though, to be honest, the past few days, watching Urse take such big chances facing the leviathan, and then, almost dying... Well, that hadn't been remotely *easy*.

But they'd survived. And they were together. Nothing would come between them now. They were true mates, deeply in love. Bonded on a soul-deep level. Life, for them, was going to be so good from here on out.

The rest of the world though... There were still big problems out there, including the leviathan and its minions waiting just off shore. More than that, there was the threat of Elspeth and her *Venifucus* fanatics.

If they had their way, no place—including the cove—would be safe.

So John had agreed to work in the shadows, with Cam. He believed that by doing so, he could help protect his mate, his people, and the world in general. John couldn't really talk about it to anyone right now, but he knew Urse would understand, as would his men, when the time came.

The kiss ended and Urse looked up at him, her eyes crinkling at the corners as she studied him. The smile on her face was peaceful. Content.

"Keep your secrets for now, my love. I trust you."

He gave her a light squeeze, hugging her. "That means more to me than you will ever know," he whispered near her ear. "And I will never, ever betray your trust, my sweet *strega*."

She pushed back so she could look into his eyes. "I know that, silly bear." Her teasing broke the serious mood, as did the way she stroked her hands over his body, stopping in some interesting—and exciting—places. "Now, how about we get started on making at least one of those little cubs you were talking about?"

He lifted her into his arms and strode toward the bedroom.

"I thought you'd never ask."

Their laughter echoed through the house, filling it with joy and hope for the future.

# # #

ABOUT THE AUTHOR

Bianca D'Arc has run a laboratory, climbed the corporate ladder in the shark-infested streets of lower Manhattan, studied and taught martial arts, and earned the right to put a whole bunch of letters after her name, but she's always enjoyed writing more than any of her other pursuits. She grew up and still lives on Long Island, where she keeps busy with an extensive garden, several aquariums full of very demanding fish, and writing her favorite genres of paranormal, fantasy and sci-fi romance.

Bianca loves to hear from readers and can be reached through Twitter (@BiancaDArc), Facebook (BiancaDArcAuthor) or through the various links on her website.

WELCOME TO THE D'ARC SIDE…
WWW.BIANCADARC.COM

BOOKS BY BIANCA D'ARC

TALES OF THE WERE ~ REDSTONE CLAN 1
GRIF

Griffon Redstone is the eldest of five brothers and the leader of one of the most influential shifter Clans in North America. He seeks solace in the mountains, away from the horrific events of the past months, for both himself and his young sister. The deaths of their older sister and mother have hit them both very hard.

Lindsey Tate is human, but very aware of the werewolf Pack that lives near her grandfather's old cabin. She's come to right a wrong her grandfather committed against the Pack and salvage what's left of her family's honor—if the wolves will let her. Mostly, they seem intent on running her out of town on a rail.

But the golden haired stranger, Grif, comes to her rescue more than once. He stands up for her against the wolf Pack and then helps her fix the old generator at the cabin. When she performs a ceremony she expects will end in her death, the shifter deity has other ideas. Thrown together by fate, neither of them can deny their deep attraction, but will an old enemy tear them apart?

Warning: Frisky cats get up to all sorts of naughtiness, including a frenzy-induced multi-partner situation that might be a little intense for some readers.

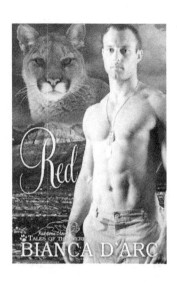

TALES OF THE WERE ~ REDSTONE CLAN 2
RED

A water nymph and a werecougar meet in a bar fight… No joke.

Steve Redstone agrees to keep an eye on his friend's little sister while she's partying in Las Vegas. He's happy to do the favor for an old Army buddy. What he doesn't expect is the wild woman who heats his blood and attracts too much attention from Others in the area.

Steve ends up defending her honor, breaking his cover and seducing the woman all within hours of meeting her, but he's helpless to resist her. She is his mate and that startling fact is going to open up a whole can of worms with her, her brother and the rest of the Redstone Clan.

TALES OF THE WERE ~ REDSTONE CLAN 3
MAGNUS

A tortured vampire, a lonely shifter, and a deadly power struggle of supernatural proportions. Can their forbidden love prevail?

Magnus is the quiet brother. The one who keeps to himself. But he has good reason for his loner status. Two years ago, he met a woman. Not just any woman. This woman made his inner cougar stand up and roar. Even in human form, he purred when she stroked him, a sure sign that she was his mate. And mating is a very serious thing among shifters. Too bad the lady had fangs...

Mag discovers Miranda being held captive. She's been tortured to the point of -madness. Mag frees her and takes her to his home, nursing her back to health and defying all convention to keep her with him. He doesn't ever want to let her go again, but he knows the deck is stacked against them.

When a vampire uprising threatens, Mag and Miranda are in the middle. More than just their necks are on the line when a group of vampires seek to kill them and overthrow the current Master. But they have powerful allies, and their renewed relationship has made both of them stronger than either would ever be alone.

Can they stay together forever? Or will the daylight—and their two very different worlds—tear them apart again?

WWW.BIANCADARC.COM

Made in the USA
Las Vegas, NV
10 December 2023

82474618R00118